Careful What You Wish For

Michelle Escamilla

Careful What You Wish For

Limitless Publishing, LLC
Kailua, HI 96734
www.limitlesspublishing.com

Formatting: Limitless Publishing

ISBN-13: 978-1-68058-237-6
ISBN-10: 1-68058-237-2

Dedication

To my amazing husband, Hoss.
You are my happily ever after.

Chapter One

"You've got this, Harley," I breathed while looking at my reflection in the mirror. I had been stressing about this day for six months. Today, I was giving the biggest presentation of my career to the board of directors. Not only had this meeting been postponed, rescheduled, and moved around, but now they had a new board member, Ethan Prince. His smile alone made my heart jump out of my chest. He said hi to me once, and I thought I was going to giggle myself to death. I was convinced that he thought I was insane by all the stuttering and laughing I did around him. Truth was, he was the only guy I acted this way around.

I stepped out of the office bathroom, hurrying to my desk. The meeting was in fifteen minutes and I still had to print out the report.

"Harley!" Lucy whispered excitedly from her cubicle next to mine. "Are you all set?"

"I think I'm going to be sick, but yes!" I shrieked. She and I had been office buddies for the last few months. I had been promoted five months ago from personal assistant to executive assistant, and was now an executive assistant in marketing. What did that mean for me? I went from copy girl to working on promotions. I wasn't a full marketing associate, but today would be the day that I might get my chance.

"You'll be fine. Just don't giggle at Ethan and I think you'll be fine," she joked. She had been walking with me when I made myself look like an idiot. Lucy sat back down at her desk and hummed along with the mini speaker on her desk.

"Oh, shut it," I laughed. I clicked on the 'print' icon on my computer and waited for my printer to work. I heard a loud beep come from the old printer and my stomach churned. "Oh shit! I'm out of ink? How the hell did I run out of ink?"

"What's wrong?" Lucy asked, standing back up.

"Do you have ink in your printer?" I was panicking now.

"Uh, I think so. Why?" she asked, looking at me strangely.

"Hannah, can you come to the conference room?" Harold requested, walking by my desk. Harold Thompson had been my boss since I received the promotion, and no matter how many times I corrected the man, he still got my damn name wrong. I was named after a damn motorcycle! How did you get that wrong?

"Y—yes, sir, but my…"

He quickly interrupted me. "Now. We haven't got all day for this."

I nodded, grabbing the notes I did have. "Wish me luck," I whispered to Lucy and she gave me a thumbs-up. As I walked up to the conference room, I saw the members of the board, the client, and Mister Dimples himself. He was the youngest male in the room at thirty-four. His chestnut-colored hair was spiked up today, rather than slicked to the side. His honey-brown eyes glistened under the florescent lighting. I tried to maintain eye contact with the client so I wouldn't sound like a complete bumbling idiot.

"Good morning, everyone," I greeted, taking a seat at the end of the long table. "I'm Harley Simpson, and I've been assigned to your account." Before I could continue, Ethan nonchalantly motioned for me to stand up. I could feel my cheeks blush, but I quickly rose to my feet. I began to give my speech on the new wine cooler that was to be released next week. They didn't have any sort of idea on what to do as a big release. I was utterly speechless that they thought it was going to be the next big thing, but had no marketing plan—that's where I came in. The drink was supposed to go on the shelves last month, but after several meeting postponements, they finally allowed me to take on the project. "So, I think that we can really get this out to the public by holding a big release party where the only drinks served will be the wine coolers. I have a couple of venues that are really interested in hosting."

Looking around the room, the clients were nodding in agreement. I couldn't be prouder of myself as I looked at the smiles around the room. Then, I had to look at Ethan. He was smiling, not at the clients, like the rest of the board members, but at me. My eyes widened, and I tried to calm myself and just give a small smile. The clients began to speak with the other board members and I soon found myself lost in a daydream with Ethan being the main star. I could hear mumbles in the background, but couldn't make any sense of it with Ethan Prince shirtless, feeding me chocolate-covered strawberries.

"Thank you, Hannah. Do you have the information of all the vendors and venues for us to look over?" Harold asked, snapping me back to reality. The clients seemed to be rather happy and were shaking hands with everyone at the table.

"We look forward to working with you," Ethan said, shaking one of the client's hands.

Fuck. Why did he have to ruin my dream? "I seem to have left it on my printer, sir. I will…I'll be right back." I nearly tripped on my heel as I turned to head out of the conference room. I ran down the hall to my desk.

"Was it that bad?" Lucy asked.

"Give me your ink!" I pleaded.

Lucy's eyes widened as she searched her printer for her cartridge. "I don't know how to get it out!"

I ran around the cubicle wall and opened her printer, grabbing the small ink box and dashing back to my printer. "Get your lil ass in there. Yeah, that's right! Work for mama, you sweet…" Just as I was about to continue sweet-talking my printer, I heard a man clear his throat behind me. I turned to find Ethan standing by the corner of my cubicle. I felt my heart stop and my palms go sweaty; I was completely mortified to see him smirking at me.

"Am I interrupting anything?" he chuckled.

I wished I could die, right then. "Uh, no, sir. I just...never mind."

"Harley, right?" he asked. I gave a slight nod. "The clients had to head out, but they were very impressed by your presentation. They want you to handle all of the arrangements for the party. Do you think you could have everything ready for this upcoming weekend?"

"Yes!" I shouted a little too excitedly. "I mean, yes, I can."

"Great. If you can have that report to me by the end of the evening, I'd appreciate it. I already told Harold you'll handle it, so all of your questions or updates need to come to me directly." He smiled and the moment that dimple on his cheek appeared, I was in lust.

"Thank you, Mr. Prince," I said quietly.

"Please, call me Ethan," he insisted, giving Lucy a smile before walking away.

I collapsed into my chair and resumed breathing, just as my printer began to print my report.

"You got the account?" Lucy asked, running to my cubicle. I nodded excitedly. "That's awesome! You even get to work with Ethan! That's the best part." She winked and nudged my arm.

That was the part that made me the most nervous. Being that close to a man I'd had many daily fantasies about was going to drive me insane or make me feel like I was slightly obsessed with the man. My office phone startled me out of my daze. "Harley Simpson," I answered.

"Hiiiii," screeched Olivia. She had been my best

5

friend since both of our boyfriends had broken up with us during our sophomore year of college. I lived vicariously through her when she was being wild and crazy. I liked to play things safe and follow the rules. Olivia Miller, on the other hand, enjoyed partying with all the frat guys and drinking. She helped me discover makeup and designer clothes, even when I was living paycheck to paycheck. "Girls night out, tonight!"

"Liv, it's Wednesday." I sighed. The last time I went out for ladies night, I woke up an hour late for work and thought hell would have been a paradise retreat compared to what I felt like.

"Best night to go out! Half-priced drinks at the Olive Room!"

I sighed as I contemplated the martinis there. They were the best, but my mind was on the project. "All right, maybe *one* drink. I did get the Tipsy's account."

"*What?*" she screeched. I pulled the phone away from my ear, letting the ringing subside. "That's great! Then yes! We're definitely going out!"

I chuckled. "All right. Seven?"

"We'll see you there! Megan and Lana will be there too!" Olivia quickly hung up and I placed the handset back down. I rolled my eyes at the thought of seeing Megan and Lana. The Knit-Whit Twins, as I referred to them, were friends of Olivia and truly the most fake people I'd ever met. They came from money and I don't think they'd ever worked a day in their lives. Daddy still paid for everything and they were nearing thirty. It actually made me sick that I had to save for three months for my

Coach purse and they could drop three months of my salary in a day. I tried to be civil with them, but the moment they started bragging about meeting Jared Leto and having dinner with Leo like it was no big deal—I couldn't be around it.

I realized the report was still sitting on my printer, Olivia's call had completely distracted me. I snatched the pile of papers and walked quickly toward the elevator. Ethan's office was only two floors above mine, yet it felt so high class having to go up there.

As I stepped off the elevator, I rounded the corner to see Ethan sitting at his oak desk, on his phone. The sun beat down in his corner office and made his brown eyes seem lighter than earlier as he looked up from his computer screen and ended his call. I had the slight urge to turn and go back, but he looked up as I began to turn away. He waved me into his office and my heart began to speed up.

"Harley, is that the report?" he asked, hanging up the phone.

"Y—yes, sir. I should've had it to you earlier, but I...well, I finally got my printer working."

He smirked up at me as I handed him the packet of papers. I could feel my legs begin to shake as his thumb hit my fingertips. What was I, fifteen?

"You're going to have to let go, Harley," he suggested, pulling the papers I apparently still had a death grip on.

"Oh, sorry. Well, back to the grind." I turned on my heels, nearly tripping over a fray in the carpet. I gritted my teeth and left his office.

"Oh, Harley," he called. I turned, and dashed

back in.

"Yes?"

"I'm going to be attending a dinner tomorrow night for another client. Would you care to join me?" he asked, smiling.

I nearly fainted. "Yes! I'd like that very much."

"Great. Dinner is at six thirty, a little early for my taste, but I'll have a car here at the office."

I nodded, smiling widely, then hurried out of the office before I could make an ass out of myself. On the elevator ride back to my floor, I made a mental note not to have more than one drink tonight, because I couldn't be looking like a zombie tomorrow.

***

I worked through the rest of the day without any sort of screw ups, even when Ethan passed me as I walked to the break room. I decided to stay a bit late tonight, rather than driving all the way to my place and then back into the city to meet the girls for drinks. I really wanted to live in downtown San Francisco, but the rent was just out of my reach. I found some great apartments thirty minutes away from work, but the traffic was never something I was excited to deal with on a daily basis. So, I traded in my car for a BART pass, which saddened me. In Iowa, I drove everywhere, but the parking was outrageous.

As I gathered the last of my things, I waited for the elevator. My heart sank into my stomach as the doors opened and I saw Ethan standing in the car with a beautiful blonde woman. Her boobs screamed, 'Look at me, I cost five thousand dollars!' But she was gorgeous. Just like him. I was an idiot for thinking he'd go for a B cup, with natural blonde hair. He nodded at me like I was an acquaintance and it made me feel sick to my stomach. Only twenty floors until I could run out of there.

Stepping out, I hurried out to a cab that was dropping someone off on the corner. The blonde had made kissy sounds the entire ride down and made me want to puke on her Louboutins. I slid across the backseat of the cab. "The Olive Room, please," I requested to the cab driver.

"You all right back there?" she asked. I had to admit, I was actually pretty impressed that it was a woman driver.

"Yeah, just...the guy that I thought was kinda interested in me at work. I think I just got my hopes up."

"Huh, was he the one with the blonde?" she asked curiously. I nodded, pulling out my phone. I sent a quick text to Olivia to let her know I was on my way. "Well, you're definitely a lot prettier than her."

"Thanks."

At a red light, the cab driver turned and faced me. "What did you think would happen?"

"Excuse me?" I gave her a puzzled look. "Like, did I think we were going to get married? Kids?" I laughed.

"Yeah, why not?" she asked.

"The light is green," I said, pointing ahead. She

didn't move. "Yeah, I had a daydream that we'd get married and have kids, I guess. He's gorgeous, and who wouldn't?" A horn blared behind us, startling me. "Can we go?"

She nodded, and continued the drive. "So, you want all that?" she asked again.

"Look, I guess I hoped that I wouldn't be almost thirty and single with no kids. My birthday is next week and it's really starting to get to me. I'd take any guy that was worthy, but Ethan Prince—yeah, he's the one I've thought about the most."

We pulled up to the bar and she turned, smiling. "Well, good luck, young lady. Oh! Happy early birthday."

I slipped her a twenty, and opened the car door. "Thanks." That, by far, was the weirdest cab ride ever. I grew up in a small town and was happy to talk to just about everyone. When I moved to San Francisco for school, I quickly learned that nobody wanted to hear your story or talk to you, unless you were friends with them or worked together. California was too busy to listen to your sob story of turning thirty and not being married.

Olivia was waiting outside the door, smoking her cigarette. "Hey, I'm so glad you could make it!" she greeted. Olivia has lived in California her entire life and helped me adapt to the major culture shock. "The twins are on their way, but we should go in. I got us a table earlier."

Olivia had married a few years ago and quickly became pregnant. She was a stay-at-home-mom to a little girl, Tabitha. She tried to tell me it wasn't all it was cracked up to be, but she was on cloud nine since she had her. Her marriage was even a fairytale, they had been together forever, it seemed like, and every time she looked at him—you could tell she was incredibly happy.

We walked into the busy bar and sat down at her favorite table. We seemed to have become regulars here. The chairs were more like ottomans that were never sold at the furniture store down the road and the tables were mismatched, but it was one of the busier bars. Their martinis were unlike anywhere else.

Our waiter, whom I'd never seen in here before, rushed over to us. "Hi, ladies," he greeted. His piercing blue eyes stood out from behind his glasses. "I'm Matt. What can I get ya?"

"Well, Matt, it'd be just *fantastic* if you could get us two dirty Grey Goose martinis," Olivia ordered. Olivia didn't take well to new waiters. Each time we came here we had Xavier, a waiter that Olivia lusted over. We knew she would never do anything with him, but she was always a big flirt with him.

"Thank you," I added with a smile.

"So, it's someone's birthday coming up next week," Olivia said in a sing-song voice. I rolled my eyes and nodded. "Are we going out?"

I shrugged, but didn't answer as Matt arrived with two martinis. "Here ya go," he said, handing us the glasses.

Olivia quickly took a sip and cringed. "Matt, is it?" He nodded at her. "This is not dirty enough. Are you planning on being a waiter here for a while?"

I felt mortified as he shifted on his feet. "Liv…" I started.

"No, I don't plan on being a waiter at a bar for the rest of my life." Matt chuckled. "I'm finishing up grad school, now. I am just doing this for some extra cash. In fact, I'm a teacher."

"Well, stick with the teaching. But while you're here, I'd like a *dirty* martini." She handed the glass back to him and smiled. Giving a sympathetic look, I mouthed a sorry. "Harley, you need to stop apologizing for everything. How are you going to land a husband if you're sorry for everything?"

I rolled my eyes, sipping on my drink. "Well, I was thinking that I'd get a nice guy," I snapped.

"Oh yeah, like that hot boss of yours! Oh, you said you got that account! Does that mean you'll get to know him better?"

I scowled at my martini. "Yeah, about that. He's not…he's with someone. I don't think I'd ever have a chance."

"Nonsense. I'm sure if you showed your tits a little more and wore shorter skirts, you'd get his attention real quick." Olivia laughed.

The thing about Olivia's comment, she wasn't kidding. She felt that was the way to land a guy—showing more skin and flirting heavily. Matt returned with another martini and winked at me. "I'd like to get to know our waiter a bit more," I said, watching Matt return to the bar.

"No! He's a waiter! You'd be back living like a college student!" Olivia retorted.

"What? He's a teacher!"

"Even worse. You need a CEO or, oh, I want to

try and set you up with our lawyer. He's a really great guy, but he's kinda going bald."

"Great…"

Olivia stood, waving at the twins as they walked in the bar. This night was getting worse by the moment. I slammed my martini and held up the glass, signaling at Matt. He nodded, and I greeted the twins. So much for just one drink.

I sat quietly as the girls chatted about new vacation plans, men they'd slept with, and designer sales. Matt eventually brought my third martini and I drunkenly looked up at him. "Thanks, sweets," I slurred.

"I'm going to call you a cab," he whispered. I nodded and slowly stood up.

"Girls, I have an early morning. I'll see y'all later." They groaned at me, but I was too drunk and too fed up with their stories to stay any longer. Matt walked me out to the cab, and as he helped me into the backseat, he slipped me his number.

"Give me a call. We'll have some coffee sometime," he said, smiling. I tried to seductively wink, but it came out as a full blink of both eyes. He shut the door and I gave the cab driver my home address. I rested my head against the cool window and began to doze off. The thought of Ethan's breathtaking smile and sparkling eyes began to cloud my brain.

Chapter Two

"Mommy! Cassie took Mister Cuddles from me and won't give him back!" A blood curdling scream woke me from my sleep. I peeked out of my right eye to notice I was no longer in the back of a cab. I was terrified, hoping the cab driver didn't take me home with him. Suddenly, I was being shaken by little hands. "Mommy? Did you hear me?"

My head shot up and I saw a little girl with tiny ringlets of hair covering her face. She resembled me when I was young. I sat and stared at the young girl as she stomped her foot at me and crossed her arms.

"Well, go get it back," I said, not knowing what else to say to her. She excitedly turned around and ran out of my room. My head felt like it was in the middle of a church bell.

"Good morning, gorgeous," a male voice said. Then I saw someone turning the corner of the bathroom in a white bath towel. "Have fun with the girls last night?" He walked into the closet and dropped the towel, grabbing a pair of boxers from a drawer. I couldn't see his face right away, but the

14

body was amazing.

I quickly covered my eyes, turning my head. "What are you doing?" I gasped.

"Getting ready for work. I thought I'd get the girls up and let you sleep a little longer. I saw that Cassie has a ballet recital tonight, but I have to meet with Alana about the Tipsy's third location celebration." The voice rang familiar, so I slowly removed my fingers from my eyes and saw Ethan Prince standing in front of me, giving me a puzzled look.

I shook my head. "Third location? I thought they were just getting started?" I didn't know if I was more shocked that I just saw Ethan's ass or that he was now talking to me about my newest client opening a third location. It was just yesterday I was talking to them about their launch party.

"What did you drink last night? They've been a big hit for a while now. When you did their first launch, it was amazing."

I sat in bed, looking around the large bedroom. I began to panic when I thought of that gorgeous blonde I had seen him walk out of the office building with. Was this their home? The mint green comforter felt cool against my skin as I pulled it up over my head. I tried to catch my breath, but each time I began to panic even more.

"Mommy's playing hide and seek again!" I could hear a shout under the blanket. I pulled it off my head and was completely confused, and in shock, when two young girls came running into the room. The younger one, who woke me up with her screaming, came in after an older one holding a

15

ratty bunny that looked like the one I had as a child. "Oh shit, that's mine!" I screeched, grabbing it from the girl.

"Oooo, Mommy said shit, again!" the youngest mocked.

"Leila said shit too!" Cassie laughed.

"Hey, both of you watch your mouths!" I shouted. The two of them ran out of the room, laughing.

"Ethan, what the hell is going on?"

"It's the same thing that goes on every Thursday morning. You get up, take the girls to school, and then do your…" he paused and waved his arms around the room, "…wifely duties, I guess."

I suddenly felt nauseous and ran into the bathroom. I'd never puked so much in my life, and I didn't remember having anything pink to drink. I rinsed my mouth and face off before returning to the bedroom. Wife? Mom? What the hell was going on?

I walked into the hallway to see frames of pictures scattered along the walls. As I slowly made my way down the stairs, I noticed a couple of items that looked familiar—my couch was here and a set of porcelain doll heads that my grandmother had left me were on the wall. I stopped in the middle of the living room and noticed there were toys scattered all around the hardwood floor.

As I walked into the massive kitchen, Ethan called out from the garage a goodbye before speeding out of the drive. The two little girls were sitting at the bar, watching me.

"Mommy, I want some cereal for breakfast,"

Leila requested.

"Can I have some coffee?" Cassie asked.

My eyes darted at her. "How old are you?"

"Six," she said matter-of-factly.

"I'm four!" Leila offered excitedly, holding up her little hand.

"Then no. How about a Pop Tart?" I offered, pouring myself a cup of coffee.

"How about some eggs?" she countered.

I hadn't made eggs in well over ten years. I had no idea if I even remembered how to make them, but I gave her a nod. I searched the entire kitchen for a pan before Cassie showed me another cabinet in the island in the middle of the kitchen, stacked with pans. Both of the girls gave me weird stares as I grabbed a bowl from another cabinet.

"Are you hungover?" Cassie asked.

"What?" I asked, surprised. First asking for coffee and now if I was hungover?

"Portia's mom is always hungover when she goes out with her friends. Are you?"

I tossed the egg shell into the garbage can and turned to her. "Yeah, I guess I am. And I'm a bit confused at what's going on." I stopped myself before I went into anything else. I whipped the eggs and dumped them into the hot pan on the stove. I had lusted over the guy, never really gotten to know him, and here I was cooking eggs for a child that was apparently mine. God, and *his*! I'd never seen him naked before today and I now had children with him! That meant I had *sex* with Ethan Prince! What the hell was going on?

"Cereal, please," Leila ordered. I quickly moved

around the kitchen and poured a large bowl of Lucky Charms and poured milk to cover the marshmallows. She looked at me in shock. "That's too much!"

"Sorry," I said, returning to the eggs. They were cooking faster than I was used to. I tried to keep things clean in the kitchen, but ended up getting slimy eggs all over the stove.

"They're all burned!" Cassie pouted.

"No, they are just cooked really, really well." I took a sip of my coffee and leaned my head against the stainless steel fridge. "What time do you have to be at school?" I groaned.

"Ten minutes ago!" Cassie laughed before taking a bite of the eggs.

"What?" I screeched. "Let's go then! Hurry!" I set my mug down and hurried them into the garage. As I pushed the girls through the doorway, Cassie and Leila stopped and turned toward me. "What's wrong? Get in the car!"

"You forgot our backpacks!" Cassie whined. The shock on their faces was almost like they were told Santa wasn't real.

"Well, where are they?"

Cassie huffed and pushed her way past me. "I'll get them." I stood in shock as I watched this sassy little girl stomp by and walk into the house. Leila crossed her arms and looked at me strangely. I opened the garage door and my heart dropped a little to see a white minivan waiting for us in the drive. I had vowed to never have a minivan and here I was about to drive one. "Seriously? A minivan? What the…?" I muttered under my breath.

Cassie struggled out the door carrying the backpacks, one over each shoulder. I stood watching as she helped Leila into her seat and tossed the bags into the backseat.

"Do...do you need any help?" I asked, but hoped they didn't need any help with the car seat buckle. I had seen one once, and thought it looked like an unsolvable puzzle box. There were so many straps and buckles. She shook her head as I closed the door.

The girls giggled and both excitedly cheered to go. Starting the car, the radio blared some children's song and my head began to pound even more. "Can we listen to the *Frozen* soundtrack again?" Leila begged. My eye began to twitch and the girls screeched along with the song.

I backed out of the driveway and hurried down the road, trying to figure out why the neighborhood looked familiar. It was the neighborhood that I had driven through several times after work and hoped that one day I'd own a home around. I felt as if I were driving in circles as we passed several houses that looked the same.

Speeding down the road, my head in a fog from everything, I guess I didn't realize how fast I was really going. Lights began to flash in my rearview mirror and a siren blared at me. "Oh no! I forgot my wallet!" I whispered.

Leila began to cry. "I don't want you to go to jail!"

I turned around in my seat. "Why would I go to jail? Am I wanted or something?" I panicked, rolling down my window.

"Good morning, miss. Do you know why I'm pulling you over?" the police officer asked.

I began to breathe heavily. "I was speeding, but officer—I'm in a bind, I—I seem to have woken up in the wrong place, I—I have these girls to get to school and..." I began to tear up as I tried to calm my breathing.

"Miss, have you been drinking?" he asked.

"What? N—no. I went out last night, and then I woke up in this house and they are saying I'm their mommy. Officer..."

"I'm going to need you to step out of the car," he commanded. The girls were beginning to weep in the backseat. I unbuckled my seatbelt and stepped out of the van. "I understand the stress of being a parent," he said. We stepped to the front of the van and he looked at me, a bit worried. "But you really need to not have a breakdown in front of your kids. I see it all too much around here. Just take a deep breath, things will get better. Slow things down and drive carefully," he said. We walked back to my side of the van and he opened my door.

I gave him a puzzled look. I kind of wanted him to arrest me so I could have a moment to figure out, or even find out, what the hell was going on. Maybe even speak to a detective to solve this shit. I slid back into the van and buckled my seatbelt.

"Officer?" I called as he walked back to his car.

"Yes, ma'am?"

"I...I must've gotten turned around. Can you possibly point me in the direction of the elementary school?"

"Miss, are you sure you haven't been drinking?"

I sighed. "I'm sure. I just…" I paused a moment to think of some sort of lie, "…I have a migraine." The officer nodded, and pointed just down the road to the school a few blocks away. He returned to his car and I pulled at the seatbelt across my lap before gripping the steering wheel.

"That was some awesome acting, Mommy!" Cassie laughed.

I shook my head, and pulled up to the curb of the school and hurried out of the van. "Okay, well I guess this is your school?" I asked, helping the girls out of the backseat.

"Don't forget to pick us up!" Cassie shouted, running up to the school doors. Leila stood next to me and held my hand.

"Don't you go to school here?" I asked.

She nodded. "You have to take me in. You always do!" I turned and looked at my reflection in the windows of the van. My hair was everywhere, makeup was smeared under my eyes, and my yoga pants possibly had half of the eggs I tried to make Cassie on them. "Look, there's Mr. Garner!" she screeched, letting go of my hand. "Hi, Mr. Garner!"

I turned to see the same piercing blue eyes from last night. "You!" I seethed.

"Good morning, Mrs. Prince," he responded, stepping back.

"You did something to my drink last night, you piece of sh—"

He interrupted me before I could continue with any sort of foul language. "Leila, why don't you head inside. Miss Patrick should be in there, tell her that I need to talk to your mommy, okay?"

Leila nodded and hugged my leg before skipping up the school stairs.

"Are you okay?" he asked as soon as Leila was out of sight.

"You roofied my drink, didn't you?" I wagged my finger at him.

"Mrs. Prince…"

"It's just Harley." I didn't even know where to begin on that whole last name situation.

"All right, I haven't worked in a bar in a long time. I certainly can say that I've never slipped anything into anyone's drink, either. "

My stomach churned again, I thought I was going to be sick. "I—I'm sorry. It's been a weird morning. All of this…" I swung my arms around to motion to the school and the van, and knocked his cup of coffee out of his hands. "Oh shit!"

"Mis…Harley, it's okay. Why don't you head home and take some time to relax," he insisted, smiling. As he bent down to pick up his cup he gave me a wink, the same one I swore was from last night.

I nodded and sighed as I walked back to the car. Now if only I could remember which house was mine.

***

When I finally found my house, using the garage door opener as a helpful tool, I ran in and laid down on the couch. I was hoping that when I closed my eyes and fell asleep, I'd wake up from this hellish nightmare.

Trying that for nearly an hour, nothing seemed to change. I walked around the house, looking at pictures from what seemed to be my beautiful wedding and the pictures of both of the girls as babies. I had some research to do, because I had no idea when they were even born.

I gasped at pregnancy pictures, and was thankful that I had lost most of that weight. As I tried to piece together everything, I heard a ringing coming from upstairs. I ran up into the bedroom I had woken up in and reached inside a purse, grabbing a cell phone.

"Hello?" I answered.

"We are *so* not drinking again!" Olivia grumbled.

"Oh my God! Liv!" I began to tear up. "What happened last night?"

"We went out to celebrate. Were you really that drunk?" she answered, confused.

"Celebrate? Please say this is a horrible joke that I'm in right now," I begged, lying down on the bed. The cool down comforter felt incredibly good on my back.

"Joke? I'm so confused. We were celebrating my divorce, silly. I'm now a single lady!"

"You're divorcing Ken?" I gasped.

"Ken? What date are you living in? I finally divorced Xavier! I will tell you, though, when you have your second divorce, you learn some tricks of the trade."

"Olivia, when…when did you marry Xavier?" I tried to think of when we'd had any sort of conversation that she was going to leave Ken.

23

"Well, you're obviously still drunk. I'm going to go and make a Bloody Mary, I think you should do the same. I'll talk to you later! Kisses!" She rushed off and hung up the phone on me. There was no way that I could have drank myself into a coma, had kids, and missed all this! Did I wake up in some alternate universe?

"That's it! I've been abducted by aliens!" I shouted. I smacked my forehead to get that crazy thought out of my head. The sound of the doorbell scared me and I ran downstairs, almost tripping on a stuffed animal lying in the middle of the stairs. I opened the door to see a red-headed lady standing on the stoop with a smirk, holding a cigarette in one hand. Her eyes were almost a violet color as they twinkled at me. I couldn't help but look her up and down—she was wearing some black pleather leggings, leopard heels, and a bright red shirt that was tied in the front. She reminded me of one of the women from *Absolutely Fabulous*. "Can I help you?" I asked.

"Hi, Harley," she greeted, tossing her cigarette to the ground.

"Wait, how do you know my name?" I asked, looking at her, puzzled.

"May I come in, dear? I think we should talk." I opened the door wider and guided her in, closing the door as she looked at the pictures on the wall. "I know this is all a little sudden."

"I'm sorry, I'm a little lost. It's been a *very* confusing morning. Can I get you some coffee?" I offered, emptying the old filter and pulling out a fresh one.

"That'd be nice," she replied, taking a seat at the bar. She quickly stood to pull some leftover cereal off the chair. "Do you not remember me?"

I turned to her after filling the coffee maker with water and pressing 'on.' I stared at her face and tried to remember where she would be from. Then it hit me. She was the cab driver. "Oh. My. God! It was *you!*" I shouted. "You did something to me on the cab ride over to the bar and it took me…No, that's crazy. What happened? How did you know I was here?"

She had a remorseful look on her face as she nodded. "We had a little mess up," she confessed. "When we spoke last night, I was about to grant a wish, but…"

"Wait, grant a wish? I'm so confused!"

"Honey, I'm your fairy godmother."

I began to laugh hysterically as I took a seat across from her. "You're joking, right?"

"I'm afraid not. Last night, I granted your wish, but then I realized after further review—you didn't, in fact, say 'I wish.' So, we have a little problem."

"You *think!*" I shouted, standing up. "I have a husband whom I've never been on a date with! I've never even kissed him and *now*, I have *two* damn kids! That, to me, is defying all science! And you're in this kitchen, which apparently is mine, saying *we* have a problem? You seem to be just fine! I think it's *me* that has a problem!"

"Harley, please calm down. We can fix this."

I sat down, and took a deep breath. This, by far, was the best news I had heard all morning. "How?" I asked anxiously. "I need to get back to my life.

And if this is how it's supposed to be, I want to do it the right way," I rambled.

"It's…" She sighed, shaking her head. "Harley, it's not that simple. I've never reversed a wish before. Granting them is easy, but actually going through and taking someone's wish away, well, I've never heard of it being done," she said solemnly.

I began to tear up. "I did want this, but in a whole different way. I don't even know if I'm happy or who my own kids are. How long am I going to have to be here?"

"It's hard to say."

I jumped up again. "That's it! My birthday! Can I wish for my life back? I can have a whole new wish!"

She shook her head. "I'm not sure it'll work like that. It might work to ask for a reverse wish. How about we plan on that and I will work on fixing this in the meantime."

I nodded my head. "Okay, so I have a week to live here?"

"Yes. Just think, you might even like this life!" she exclaimed. I gave her a knowing look. "Well, you might. You did say that you wanted all this!"

"I know I did. This is just very…soon!"

"I'll keep in touch and we can meet up if I have a solution. If not, well, there's always your birthday."

I walked her to the door and opened it up for her. "I don't even know your name."

"It's Donna. Donna Corleone."

I tried to hold back the laughter. "You're serious?" I snickered. She glared at me. "Isn't that like…?"

Donna quickly interrupted, "Yes, I know. My parents apparently had a sense of humor." She turned, and headed to the car that was parked along the curb.

I shut the door, and slouched down. "This couldn't be that bad, right?" I whispered to myself.

Chapter Three

Soon after Donna left, I fell asleep on the floor. The hardwood flooring was surprisingly comfortable, and nothing could feel worse than the hangover I had earlier. One whiff of my breath, and I knew it was time for me to get up and attempt to get ready.

As I brushed my teeth, I walked into the closet to pick out some clothes. I figured being married to the CEO of one of the top marketing firms in California, the selection of clothing was going to be amazing.

"Where's the Chanel? The Michael Kors?" I whispered, browsing through the tenth pair of yoga pants. I hurried into the bathroom and tossed my toothbrush onto the sink, grabbing the house phone off the charger next to the bed. Scrolling through the contacts on the phone, I quickly selected Ethan's work number.

"Hi, feeling better?" he answered.

"Where the hell are all my clothes?" I seethed. Granted, I didn't own any Chanel before this, but I didn't own more than two pairs of yoga pants, either. I didn't even *do* yoga.

"Sorry? Last I saw, they were in the closet. Did someone rob us while you were out?" he joked.

"Not funny! Since when did I give up on myself?" There was an awkward silence. I waited another moment until I realized that it was all me. "Never mind. I was thinking I might go to the mall later."

"Really? All right, have fun. I need to work a little late tonight, but I'll see you later?"

My stomach filled with nervous butterflies. He really was sweet and I began to think that maybe this whole messed up wish wasn't so bad after all. I slipped into one of the jean skirts from the closet shelf and grabbed one of the many tank tops, trying to make the best of what I had at the moment.

Finishing up with my hair, the phone began to ring. I grumbled as I walked into the bedroom to pick it up. "Hello?" I answered.

"Mrs. Prince, this is Gayle down at the school."

"Uh-huh."

"Well, it's three forty-five."

I wished this woman would tell me what was going on. "Okay?"

"Mrs. Prince, school was let out twenty minutes ago; your girls are in the office waiting for you to pick them up. Was there an emergency?" she said in a huff.

"Oh shit! All right, I'm on my way down! I'm so sorry!" I hung up the phone and tossed it on the bed, then ran down the stairs. I was horrible at this mother thing. How these kids made it to six and four was beyond me.

I got in the car, and sped down the road. As I rounded the corner, I realized flashing lights were in my rearview. Again. I pulled off to the side, and sighed.

"Afternoon, do you…Again? Lady, you gotta slow it down," the officer sighed.

"Officer, I want to thank you for letting me off and giving me the pep talk this morning. It has been a rather off day for me."

"Well, this time, I'm going to have to give you a ticket," he said, pulling a pen from his shirt pocket.

"I understand. I'm just late for picking up my girls." I hoped the guilt-trip would stop him from writing, but that didn't seem to faze him.

"License and registration," he ordered. I searched the car for my purse and realized I was in a hurry, yet again, and had left without any sort of wallet or purse.

"Umm, Officer, I seem to have left my purse at home," I said sweetly.

He shook his head, and even behind his aviator glasses I could see him squeezing his eyes shut, almost as if I was giving the poor man a headache. "This is the last time. Go get your kids, and slow it down."

I nodded quickly. "Yes, sir! Thank you," I paused and checked his badge for his name, "Officer Carter, so much!"

He moved away from the van and I pulled away from the curb to make it down to the school. When I pulled up, the girls were sitting on the stairs with Leila's teacher. I jumped out of the driver's seat and hurried toward them.

"Mommy!" Leila exclaimed excitedly.

"You forgot us!" Cassie shouted, storming past me. I felt horrible.

"Girls, I said your mom didn't forget about you. Hi, Harley," Matt greeted, smiling.

"Hi. I'm really sorry about this morning." I couldn't stop staring at his sparkling eyes.

"It's not a problem, but if you're looking for a way to make it up, we need some parent volunteers for the upcoming school dance," he hinted.

I sighed, knowing I did need to make it up to him. "All right, let me know what I can do."

"Great! I'll email you a list."

"Mom! Let's go! I have ballet tonight!" Cassie shouted from the van door. I waved goodbye to Matt and hurried to the car.

"What time is ballet?" I looked back, getting into the driver's seat.

"Seven, I think."

I looked into the rearview mirror and she had a scowl on her face. The girls looked disappointed that I didn't offer to put their music on, but I thought I would introduce them to something other than a Disney soundtrack and blasted some Justin Timberlake.

Pulling into the driveway, the girls ran into the house, tossing their backpacks on the floor and quickly turned on the TV. Just when I thought I was safe from any other annoying sounds of animated characters, the sound of SpongeBob's laugh echoed through the house.

I grabbed the remote out of Cassie's hand and

sprawled myself out on the opposite couch, changing the channel to one of the 'Who's the Baby Daddy?' daytime television shows.

"Hey! We were watching that!" Cassie shouted.

"SpongeBob will rot your brain! Don't you have homework to do?"

"Aww, man," Leila whined. Both of them grabbed their bags off the floor and walked to the table. They both started to work quietly as I browsed the long list of channels. "What's for dinner?" Leila asked as she colored on a piece of paper.

If I had to make another meal, like the egg disaster, we would surely starve. I trudged over to the kitchen and began to search the fridge and cupboards, finding nothing but healthy food. I began to wonder when I became such a health freak. My meals, before all this, consisted of cup of noodles and anything that came in a takeout container.

"Pizza?" I asked. The girls' faces lit up and I took that as a yes.

"Does Daddy know that you're ordering junk food?" Cassie asked.

I realized why I became a health nut. "No, but let's keep it a secret," I whispered, winking.

The girls began to snicker, and went back to their homework. I was beginning to redeem myself with them and it definitely felt better.

***

Forty-five minutes later, the pizza arrived and I

had never seen two little girls devour so much food. After everyone finished up, Cassie quickly changed into her black leotard and Leila changed into some sort of princess costume.

"What is that?" I asked Leila, looking her up and down.

"I'm a princess!" she exclaimed, giving a twirl.

"Yeah, ummm…why are you wearing it?"

"I wanna be a princess," she said quietly.

"Uh, I think you should go change."

She crossed her arms and scowled at me, shaking her head. "No!" she shouted.

"Leila, I'm not going to take you to your sister's dance wearing that!" I argued, crossing my arms. She wasn't going to show me up. We stood there staring at each other in a massive battle of scowls, but I felt myself slowly giving in. "Gah! Fine!" I shouted, throwing my hands in the air.

Checking the time, I realized I hadn't heard from Ethan at all since earlier this afternoon and began to wonder how things were going. Staying home was nice, but if Tipsy's was doing well, I wanted to get back to work.

"Can you do my hair?" Cassie asked, handing me a brush.

"Sure, what do you want?"

"A bun," she answered sarcastically. I guess I should have figured that's what it would be. I did ballet when I was younger too. My best attempt on a little girl bun consisted of thirty-two bobby pins. That sucker was not going to fall, even in a hurricane.

"So, where is this ballet recital?" I asked the girls

33

as they slipped on their shoes. Both of them shrugged.

I searched the kitchen for some sort of address or notice about this dance. I found an invitation underneath a magnet on the fridge. As I pushed the girls out the door, I dialed Ethan's number. I tried calling several more times on the way to the recital, but each time my call was directed straight to voicemail.

The girls and I arrived a little early, just to be on the safe side. Noticing we still had fifteen minutes until the recital began, I felt a little relieved I was actually early for something today. Several moms were already standing around chatting outside the little theater. I guided the girls around them, trying my hardest to avoid any sort of contact with them. I didn't know what to talk to them about.

"Mrs. Prince!" an older woman called out. I stopped in my tracks, turning to her. "Hi, I'm Cassie's dance instructor, Polly. We met the last time?"

"Oh, yes," I lied.

"I…well, I thought you were going to bring the snacks this week," she said hesitantly.

"Oh, well, uh, I'm sorry. Next week?" I offered. "What's that, honey?" I asked, leaning down to Leila. "Oh, I need to take her to the bathroom."

"I don't have to go potty!" Leila answered, looking up at me oddly.

The woman did *not* look very happy with me. She gave a polite, yet seething smile. "Sounds good." She turned and walked away from me. I scowled at Leila as we walked into the auditorium, and picked seats toward the back of the room.

Polly tiptoed onto the stage, smiling widely. "Parents, welcome! Our Little Ladybugs have been working really hard on their dance routines. Let's give them a round of applause." She clapped excitedly as the little girls piled onto the stage.

Cassie looked so cute up on the stage, and the bun was still in place. I was pretty proud of myself. As the girls set up for their third dance, I shifted in my seat. Bored, I pulled out my phone and checked to see if I had any sort of games. The girls began to dance another dance and I figured I would at least record one of them. Cassie started to look a little pale in the face when I zoomed in on her. She stopped dancing, and looked directly at me. She puked in the middle of the stage. I could hear the little screams and began to screech along with the rest of the crowd, until the dance teacher motioned for me to go up there. I hesitated several times, but cringed as I finally walked up to the stage. I held back the dry heaves as I helped her off the stage. The smell of vomit was never an easy thing for me.

"I don't think pizza was a good idea," I whispered as we walked to the car.

"My tummy hurts," Cassie groaned, climbing into the back of the van.

"That was funny!" Leila laughed. Leave it to a four-year-old to think puking akin to that scene in *The Exorcist* was funny.

"Please don't puke in the backseat," I begged. Granted it was only a minivan, but I gagged at the thought of her throwing up in the car. I'd never seen so much puke come out of someone so tiny and petite, though.

As I pulled into the driveway, I was excited to see a shiny black Lexus parked in the garage. Ethan was home and he could help with the girls. It was too much to take on for my first day as a mom. The girls hurried inside and I dragged behind. Ethan was sitting at the table going over paperwork with a beer sitting in front of him. He looked freshly showered and was wearing nothing but a pair of black basketball shorts. I, on the other hand, smelled like pizza, sweat, and vomit. I needed a long, hot shower to bring me back to normal.

I hurried over to him, impressed by his amazing build, but more for the beer that was open in front of him.

"Hey, that was mine," he said, looking at me in shock as I chugged the brew.

"Daddy! Mommy bought us pizza for dinner and Cassie puked all over the stage!" Leila shouted in a sing-song voice. I turned and glared at her, then heard a chuckle come from Ethan.

"She really puked?" he asked, worried. I nodded, taking another gulp of the cold beer.

"Oh, everywhere. It was like nothing I had ever seen before." I gagged. "Why didn't you tell me that she couldn't handle pizza?"

"Because we already discussed this months ago when she puked in the dining room." He gave me a strange look, as if I was supposed to know this.

Ethan sat back in his chair and laughed a little bit before standing up. "Girls, shower and bed time." He motioned for them to go upstairs, kissing me on the cheek as he walked by. Taking another chug of the beer as I plopped down on the couch, I was looking forward to spending time with Ethan and finding out how we ended up married.

After waiting on the couch for thirty minutes, Ethan had yet to return. I tossed the bottle in the trash, turned off the lights, and walked up the stairs to see him lying in the bed. "Hey," I said quietly.

"Oh, hey," he responded.

"I was waiting for you downstairs. I thought you'd be coming back." I climbed into the bed, snuggling down into the covers.

"Early meeting tomorrow," he said, reading something off his phone.

"Oh. I was thinking today," I started. Ethan set his phone on the nightstand next to him and faced me. "Isn't it funny how we recall stories?"

"Ummm…" Ethan laid down on his pillows and rubbed his head.

"Yeah, like how our memories tend to pick up details that the other doesn't remember." I could tell he was totally confused. "Like, how do you recall how we met?"

"Harley, are you okay?" he asked, grabbing my hand.

"Yeah, just feeling a little sentimental today," I lied.

"We worked together on several accounts and things just happened," he said, pulling me into a kiss.

"Did things turn out the way you wanted?" I asked, scooting closer to him.

"Well, I didn't think we'd have kids right away. Apparently, condoms really aren't reliable," he chuckled. My heart sank. Did he marry me because I had gotten pregnant? "But we have two really great girls and I think things are great now."

I sighed, smiling. "Oh, good."

"Well, I have an early meeting in the morning. Get some rest," he insisted, turning off the small lamp on the nightstand.

"I'm actually going to take a hot shower. I'll see you in the morning," I whispered. I crept into the bathroom and turned on the water. Besides the struggle of two kids, it seemed like everything was going to be okay here. I sat on the toilet, waiting for the water to warm up, and thought—*with a last name like Prince, he was bound to be* the one...*right?*

Chapter Four

A soft kiss on my forehead startled me awake. Ethan was leaving, and it was only six in the morning. I waved goodbye with a grunt. I had never been a morning person, and even with a whole new life, I was not about to start. Finally falling back asleep, the alarm buzzed loudly at seven. It felt like I had only slept for five more minutes. I grumbled and quickly made my way to the coffee maker. As I waited for the coffee to begin to brew, I could hear screams already starting from upstairs. I cringed at the shrills.

"Mommmmy!" Leila shouted.

"Huh," I groaned.

"I was supposed to bring cupcakes today!" she panicked.

"You *what*?" I gasped, turning to face the little girl that was standing with a big smile on her face. "How many?"

"Twenty."

I rolled my eyes, taking a deep breath and holding it in. "We'll stop at the store on our way in.

39

Hurry and get ready," I instructed, pouring a cup of coffee. There went my opportunity to attempt to look near human. As I went to check on Cassie, she came down wearing her outfit already and walked to the table. She obviously got my feelings on mornings.

"Morning," I said.

"Morning, Mommy," she muttered, laying her head on the table. "I don't want to go to school today."

"Oh, you're going to school," I quickly replied. I didn't know how I'd survive as a full-time mom. The poor girl looked like she had tears in her eyes, so I figured I could try to find out why. "But why do you want to stay home?"

"Robbie told me that I was a 'rhymes with witch' because I didn't want to be his girlfriend. Now, his friends are calling me RWW," she sobbed.

"He called you a bitch?" I shrieked. I couldn't believe kids were talking like this.

"No, just said I rhymed with witch."

"What a little asshole. Want me to talk to the little shit?"

"Please don't, it'll only make it worser," she begged. I nodded, but made a mental note to kick some little seven-year-old's ass if he called this sweet girl a bitch again.

"All right, well, if he does it again—call him a douche bag," I encouraged. She looked at me like she had seen a ghost, before she thought about it and snickered. "Want something for breakfast that does *not* include eggs?" I laughed. "We need to run by the store to pick up some cupcakes for your sister, so eat fast."

She nodded. "I'll have some cereal. I need to bring some cupcakes or something too."

Did these kids always wait until the last minute for snacks? It was a good thing they didn't expect me to bake them.

Grabbing two bowls, filling them only half way this time, I set them on the table and poured milk into one. Leila walked into the kitchen wearing leopard print tights, a zebra skirt and a bright pink shirt with a puppy on the front. I looked at her strangely as she slipped on her purple glittered tennis shoes before she made her way to the table.

"Is...is that what you're wearing today?" I asked, pouring milk into her bowl.

She excitedly nodded, stuffing a large bite of cereal into her mouth. "Yes!"

After yesterday's breakdown for wearing a princess costume to the dance recital, I was going to just go with it. Cassie had a jean skirt on with a purple tank. She matched, at least. I sighed and sipped my coffee, wondering who the hell taught these girls how to dress.

I checked the time and we still had a good thirty minutes to spare, just enough to run into the store and grab some cupcakes, and then get them to school on time. *Without getting pulled over today*, I vowed to myself.

The girls scooped their bags off the floor, and I grabbed my purse and the keys off the end table by the couch. It still killed me a little bit inside to see it wasn't my Coach that I had spent all that money on. We headed out the door and I wondered how women did this every day and still have time to shower. It was beyond me. I was only on my second day, well, of my sixth year, and I was already feeling burned out.

We pulled into the grocery store parking lot, and the girls hurried inside as I quickly followed behind. The bakery had several parents who looked like they were just notified this morning by their kids that they were to bring a treat too. A black-haired woman waved at me and rushed over.

"Did you get told this morning too?" she chuckled.

"Yep," I said, hoping she didn't expect me to know her name.

"Portia told me as we were heading out the door. I don't think we have formally met." She held her hand out for mine. "I'm Gloria. Portia talks about Cassie constantly."

"Oh, hi, I'm Harley." I shook her hand and felt relieved that we were just meeting. Leila and Cassie were over in the corner talking to a little girl that was the spitting image of the woman in front of me. Long black hair, tan skin, and dark brown eyes. They even had the same beautiful smile.

"Harley? As in the bike?" She chuckled.

"Yeah, my dad was really into Harley's, but my mom refused to let him get one. When I was born she told him, 'You wanted a Harley, here ya go.'" I laughed.

"That's awesome. Well, I guess—you bring one flavor, and I'll bring the other?" she asked, pointing to the cupcake table.

"That's a shitload of cupcakes. What is this for?"

"They want to load the kids up on sugar before they send them home. It's part of some big class party. Each class tries to celebrate once a month for all the birthdays that month."

"Ah. Well," I said, grabbing the cupcakes and handing the chocolate ones to her, "you can be the one to be blamed for the chocolate mess. Oh shit, I need to grab some cookies too. I'm going to have *two* kids high on sugar tonight." We both laughed.

"I like you. You're better than some of the other moms. Some of them are really stuck up and have no idea about small talk," she commented, taking the cupcakes. I was about to respond when I heard a loud crash. I looked over and saw Leila looking at me with wide eyes next to an empty stand, surrounded by candy bars lying on the ground.

"My cue to run. I'll catch ya later," I said as I ran over to Leila. "C'mon, let's go," I whispered, pulling her quickly away from the mess. I hurried into an empty checkout lane and handed the cashier the cupcakes and cookies. I noticed she was scowling at me as I tried to remain calm.

"Mom, aren't you going…" Cassie started. I covered her mouth and glared at her. Leila was still in shock that she had knocked a large display over. She continued to try and talk, but I kept hushing her.

"Eight thirty-seven," the cashier stated. I grabbed a ten dollar bill out of my purse, smiling. She handed my change to me, and I handed Cassie the grocery bag as I shoved the change into my little purse. I hurried the girls back to the van and vowed never to let Leila out of my sight in any sort of store again.

We pulled up to the side of the school, without being pulled over, just in time. The girls headed into their school as I stood next to the van, waving.

"Better morning?" Matt asked, walking up to me. His eyes were sparkling in the sunlight that beamed through the trees.

"Much, thanks." I smiled.

"I should have the info for the dance later on today. I appreciate the extra help, not a lot of parents like to get involved with the school activities."

"Well, I owe you for knocking your coffee out of your hand, along with making you stay late from your wife yesterday with the girls."

"I'm not married," he corrected. "It wasn't a problem. Leila and Cassie are great kids."

"Thanks," I replied. I could feel my cheeks suddenly reddening. "Well, I better let you go. I have some errands to run. I promise to be here on time today."

He chuckled and began to head into the school. "See ya later, Harley."

I turned and headed into the van, there was some major wardrobe adjustments to be made. I hadn't spent months of eating Ramen or leftovers to buy nice clothes to spend my time here in this other dimension wearing yoga pants. I hoped the credit card had a decent limit.

***

"That'll be five hundred and twenty-six dollars

and fifty-nine cents," the cashier said happily. I hesitantly handed her my credit card from my purse and inspected the other cards that were in each slot. Each read 'Harley Prince,' making me a little happier to see that I was really his wife. The cashier handed my card back to me and smiled. "Please sign here," she added, handing a pen over.

I struggled signing my last name differently, but in the end, walked out with several new pairs of shoes, tops, and cute jeans and skirts. I also had something sexy for tonight, which made me feel a little nervous, but I looked hot. After having the luxury of not having to go into work on a Friday morning and spending money on new clothes, I began to think I didn't want to go back to my other life. Grabbing a Starbucks before I left the mall, I sipped on the cold coffee and walked back to the van waiting for me in the lot. My phone began to ring inside my purse and I quickly shoved the bags onto the back seat.

"Hello?" I answered.

"Five hundred bucks?" a voice seethed.

"Ethan?"

"Who else would be calling you about five hundred bucks. Harley, I thought we discussed that your budget for clothing if you were going to continue staying home was fifty."

I nearly spit my coffee out my mouth *and* my nose. "Are you serious? I wouldn't have even gotten one pair of jeans!"

"Look, we talked about this. When you wanted that house, you agreed to cut back."

"Ethan, I…" I stopped, because I could tell this

discussion was not going to get us anywhere. "I'm sorry. I guess I could go return it."

"No," he sighed. "Is Olivia still babysitting tonight? Maybe we can discuss this over dinner."

"Dinner?" I asked excitedly.

"Well, I figured that it was date night…"

"Oh! Yes! I can't wait!" I exclaimed eagerly.

"I'll be home around six thirty. Our reservations are at seven. See you later," he said, hanging up the phone.

A night without kids and a nice dinner? Maybe a dinner out with him would help me find out if we were really supposed to be this way. So far, I had an extremely hot husband, two adorable daughters—which I still needed to get used to—and a really nice house.

As I pulled into my drive, a familiar car was parked out front. When I stepped out, Donna hurried out of the car.

"Harley!" she shouted, running up the lawn. "I think I have the solution!"

"Donna, I think…I think that I was supposed to have this life!" I responded, smiling and holding up my bags.

"Honey, you're definitely not supposed to have this life," she argued.

"Wait, how do you know?" I scowled. "Yesterday, you didn't seem to know."

"Well…" she hesitated.

I threw the bags onto the ground and raised my hands up at her, controlling the urge to strangle her. I took several deep breaths. "Donna," I began calmly. "Where the hell am I supposed to be?"

"I can't tell you. You're supposed to find it out for yourself, but Prince Charming is definitely not Ethan Prince. That's what I *can* tell you. I'm so sorry, Harley."

I reached down and picked up the bags that were sprawled along the front yard, then stomped away from Donna toward the house. "How do I get out of this, then? This is so hard, I'm really starting to like those little girls."

"I was up all night researching. You have to realize the path you are meant to take. You don't need any wishes, but once you figure it out—it will all begin to fix itself."

"So, I have to figure out that this is the life I'm not supposed to have? That's easy." I turned to her and took a deep breath in. "*This is not the life I'm supposed to have!*" I shouted at the top of my lungs. "See, I've realized it. Why aren't things going back to normal?"

"Harley, you have grown an attachment to all this. The girls. That shopping spree. You even landed the guy that you wanted. You need to *realize* that everything here may not be meant for you."

I led Donna into the living room and tossed the bags onto the floor.

"Well, what about yesterday? I realized it then!" I argued. Donna sat down on the couch and sighed. "Donna, maybe *this is* my life and you got that wrong too."

"I can assure you, it's not. Things…things aren't always what they seem. Look, you still can try to wait until your birthday, I'm sure I can have something worked out by then, but in the meantime, you're sure to find out that the life you're meant to have is not this one." Donna stood up from the couch and leaned in, giving me a hug.

"Donna, you're a horrible fairy godmother," I whispered, trying my best not to be angry. Donna nodded, leaving my house.

Thinking I had everything that I could ever want, I now had to rethink everything. I sat on the couch, my mind wandering every which way. And then my phone vibrated.

Olivia: Don't forget to bring that bottle of wine for me. Your kids are gonna want me drunk.

It never failed, Olivia still made me smile. I sent a text back, reassuring her I wouldn't forget any sort of alcohol for her. I suddenly remembered there was no way she still lived in the city and began to search frantically around the house for some sort of address for her. Digging under the couch for what appeared to look like an address book, the doorbell rang and startled me. I pushed myself off the floor and ran to the door.

"Don't make it that cheap shit either," Olivia stated, pushing her way in through the door.

"Liv, what are you doing here?" I asked, looking at her strangely.

"Well, Tabitha just left with her dad for the weekend and I figured I'd walk over here and pick out some wine before you left to get the kids."

"Wait! You live next door?" I asked surprised.

Liv gave me an odd look and continued, "Shall I order pizza tonight?"

"No!" I shouted. "Sorry, we had pizza last night, it wasn't pretty."

"I was gonna say. I know you guys are on some health kick, ever since Ethan commented on your weight, but…"

"That's why I've got my fridge stocked with healthy shit?" I screeched. "He said I was fat?" My heart dropped into my stomach. Ethan would never say something like that, would he?

Olivia laughed, and walked down the stairs into the basement. She definitely had been over here more than once. I followed her to see that I had an entire cellar of wine stocked up in the back of the basement. I made a mental note of where to find everything.

She grabbed a bottle of red wine and linked arms with me. "So, where are you two going tonight?"

"I really don't know." I grinned widely. I really didn't care to be honest—I was going on my first official date with Ethan Prince.

"Awww, you're going to get all sentimental on me now, aren't you?" she joked, walking to the door. "Bring the girls by after school and I'll make sure to feed them something somewhat healthy." She winked, and right then, I knew she was lying.

"Okay. Thanks for watching them. They've been…a handful." I sighed as I held the door open for Olivia. I looked at the time as I shut the door and realized I needed to pick up the girls.

Chapter Five

Driving down the road, I passed a police officer sitting at the stop sign ready to make a turn. I wanted to wave and point out how safe I was driving, but didn't want to press my luck. I pulled up to the school and found that I was actually early. My phone made a horrible beep and I pulled it out of my pocket to see I had an email from Matt.

Hi Harley,

I was trying to come up with all of the things that we needed to have done for the party, but rather than trying to fit them into a single email—coffee, Sunday morning? I have a packet that I could copy and give to you and we can try to wrangle in some other parents.

Thanks,

Matt Garner

I felt a little flushed. Was my daughter's teacher actually trying to hit on me? I shook my head and remembered that this was to talk about a school dance. "Don't flatter yourself, Harley," I whispered to myself. The school bell rang and I stepped out of the car. Gloria was walking up the sidewalk and politely waved.

"Hey, how do you think the cupcakes turned out?" I asked.

"I'm sure they are like crack addicts by now, trying to find their next fix. Do you think it's too soon for rehab?" she joked, chuckling.

"So, I've been conned into helping with some sort of school dance coming up. Can I bribe you into helping me out? We'd be working with Mr. Garner."

"That sexy, blue-eyed kindergarten teacher? Count me in." Gloria laughed, playfully nudging me.

"He is pretty hot," I admitted.

"Last I heard, his girlfriend left him. He is single and on the market," she stated.

"Go for him," I encouraged.

"Yeah right, I don't think that young thing could handle me." Gloria hushed up as she saw him open the door, helping the dessert-covered children out the doors. "What about you? I think he likes you!"

"I'm married," I said, holding up my left hand.

"Oh." The way she said 'oh' almost made me want to question the tone, but I left it as Leila ran up to me.

"Mommy! We had all sorts of junk food today, it was delicious and I love cupcakes. The cookies you and Cassie got this morning were so yummy," she rambled.

"Well, you were right…crack addicts," I said to Gloria, laughing. Cassie was close behind with chocolate still in the corners of her mouth. She waved excitedly as she hurried down the stairs.

"Guess what?" she asked happily.

"Robbie…he got busted calling me a…the word that rhymes with witch, and got sent to the principal's office! I didn't have to call him a douche!"

Gloria looked over at us with wide eyes. I pushed Cassie into the van and faced Gloria, blushing. "I guess she overheard me," I lied.

"Kids, they pick up on things so quickly." Gloria turned, and began to walk down the street with her daughter.

As soon as she turned away, I smacked my forehead. I was about to get in the van when I heard my name being called. I looked around and saw Matt waving.

"I just got your email," I said as he approached.

"I hope it wasn't too…inappropriate. I don't normally ask parents to join me for coffee, especially over the weekend. I just think it's a lot to go over and it would be best when the kids aren't running around screaming or when I'm trying to teach class."

"I totally agree. I'm up for coffee. So, is Sunday at ten okay? I just persuaded Portia's mom, Gloria, into helping. I didn't get a chance to ask her about coffee, though. I hope that's okay."

"Oh, yeah. I'm surprised another mom agreed!"

He seemed to be in shock.

"Do, uh, school events not get organized often?"

"They don't. I took over the planning when my gir...well, when I saw some free time open up for fundraising."

"Right. Well, I've gotta get these girls home, but I'll see you Sunday, for sure," I said, reaching for the door. His eyes sparkled at me as he waved goodbye. No matter what Olivia told me the other night, well, in my *real* life, he would have definitely been one guy that I would have wanted to get to know a little better.

***

After pulling into the driveway, I made the girls get the things that they wanted to bring over to Olivia's house and as soon as they gathered everything I followed them over. Thankfully, they knew where they were going. Olivia had already started drinking and poured me a glass as I walked through the door. Her house looked so different from the way she had it designed when I last saw her. This whole new life was so confusing. When she was with Ken, everything had been florally and bright. Now her place had turned for the complete opposite—she had dark colors everywhere, her home was a mess, and as I watched Olivia move around, it almost seemed that she was miserable as well.

"Liv," I started. She led me upstairs to her bedroom to go through her clothes. "What happened with you and Ken?"

She stopped in the doorway of her room, dropping her head. Turning to face me, she took a deep breath. "You don't remember?" she asked. I shook my head. "After you started dating Ethan, we talked and you told me that Ken should have been more attentive—how Ethan was. I thought I had everything, but when you pointed out what I was missing out on…I just left." She paused, sighing. "Xavier was a great filler, but he definitely wasn't what I wanted. I miss Ken, but I messed things up."

My heart shattered. It turned out I had ruined their marriage? I had never felt so low in my entire life. "Liv…"

She quickly interrupted, "No! I did it. It's done, and he's fine and I'm…well, I'm fine. Let's find you something amazing to wear to dinner!" She smiled and walked into her massive closet, stuffed with clothes. I took a seat on the edge of her bed and waited for her to reappear. She still had a picture of her and Ken on her dresser. "I found them!" she hollered, emerging from the back of the closet with several dresses draped over her arms.

"Wow, how many dresses do you own?" I joked.

"Well, look them over." Olivia laid the dresses out on the bed. Two black, a blue, two reds and a white dress. Each of them was a different style and I couldn't believe how many more clothes the woman had piled in her closet. I picked up one of the black and one of the red dresses and held them up to me in front of the mirror over her dresser.

"I think I'm going to go with the black. I don't want to wear anything too flashy," I said, setting the red dress on the bed.

She laughed, and sipped her wine. "You don't want flashy? Since when? You love flashy, especially after marrying Ethan, and I think I have myself to blame for it. But you love bright and attention-grabbing! You've been acting a little weird, honey. Is everything okay?"

I looked at her, a little confused—I had never liked things flashy. I was always a sideline player, never center of attention. "Liv, have you ever woken up one day and thought—this isn't my life?"

"All the damn time!" She chuckled, pointing around her room. "Uh-oh, are you and Ethan having problems again?"

"Again?" I asked. Things so far in the last couple of days seemed to be good. Donna's words, 'things don't always appear to be what they seem,' echoed through my mind.

"Well, it's been a while since your last fight. Things definitely can't get back to normal after indiscretions."

"Ethan cheated on me?" I gasped, sitting down on the bed.

"No! Well, not that I'm aware of. From what I understand, he's just working a lot, but you know when men work a lot...well, that's oftentimes their excuse. Harley, I don't think he'd cheat on you, though. You're my best friend and in all honesty, things usually get better. Now, sit down and tell me why you think this isn't your life."

"Uh." I didn't even know what to say. She was right, but in every movie I had ever watched, when a guy had to work late all the time, something was going on. I shrugged my shoulders and heard the girls running around the house. "Things are…good, I guess. I just have moments where I can't believe where we are right now. Living next door, kids, you know."

"Growing up is crazy." Liv walked out of the room to greet the girls. "Who's ready to stay up all night watching rated R movies?" I heard her ask. I shook my head and sat back down on her bed.

Donna was definitely right, this was *not* my life. I caused a divorce between my best friend and the love of her life because I was being spoiled and she wasn't? Things definitely seemed fine between Ethan and me, so it was hard to believe that we had problems in the past. I could only sit there and hope that we had resolved that issue and were finally happy. He always seemed like such a nice guy. And now, I was paranoid that he was cheating on me.

"Mommy," Cassie said, poking her head into the room. "Auntie Liv said I can have a phone when I turn nine!"

"Olivia!" I shouted. What nine-year-old needed a damn phone? I grabbed the black dress off the bed and walked downstairs. Olivia already had candy and popcorn set out on her coffee table in the living room when I turned the corner. Those lucky kids. "Liv, I'm going to go get ready. Thanks for watching them."

"Not a problem. Have fun and remember, things will get better." I waved to everyone and hurried out the door. I wanted to have super smooth legs, especially if I was potentially having sex tonight.

Chapter Six

"Man, I look hot," I said to myself, checking my reflection for the hundredth time. The time was already six forty-five. I hadn't heard from Ethan to tell me that he was running late, and I tried not to panic. I contemplated texting Olivia, but she would just fill my head with horrible ideas. He said the reservations were at seven, so if we were going to make it, he needed to be home. Now.

Pacing back and forth, I grabbed a glass from the cupboard, about to pour myself a glass of wine, when I heard the garage door opening. I returned the glass and hurried to the door.

"Where have you been?" I asked, looking at my watch.

"Work," he snapped.

"We have dinner reservations in ten minutes."

"I know. Let me go change my shirt and we can go. It'll only take me a minute." Ethan ran upstairs and I grabbed my purse, then walked out to the car. Sliding into the passenger seat, I couldn't help but think there was the smell of perfume, one other than

57

mine. Shaking my head, I tried to clear that thought out of my mind—I was becoming paranoid.

Moments later, Ethan walked out of the house in a black button-down shirt and his hair was spiked up. He looked incredibly sexy. He sat down behind the steering wheel and grabbed my hand, winking.

"You look nice," he said, driving down the road.

"Thank you. I borrowed this from Liv," I answered, smoothing out my dress. It didn't take us very long until we pulled into the parking lot of an Italian bistro. The place didn't look very packed, so the fact that we were ten minutes past our reservation time didn't look like it would make a difference. There were a couple of cars parked in the dim parking lot. The windows were stained glass with the Italian flag on each. The cloth awning was beyond worn with what looked like hail damage and rips, which made me even more skeptical of the place.

Ethan jogged around the car and opened the passenger door for me, holding my hand during the entire walk into the restaurant.

"Mr. Prince! So nice to see you again," a friendly, older man greeted. "Mrs. Prince—you're looking well!" He leaned in and kissed my cheek. "Where are the girls?"

"Hi, Anthony. It's just the two of us tonight," Ethan said, placing his hand on my lower back.

"Ah! Come, come, I've got a wonderful special meal for you." Anthony led us to a back booth. We passed a bunch of empty tables that had beautiful green table clothes, but the chairs looked as if they were about to fall apart. I was suddenly happy we were getting a booth. As we walked through the restaurant, I noticed only a few older couples dining with jeans and shorts on, it seemed very casual. Scooting into the booth, I felt a little ridiculous for having put so much effort into my outfit. I hoped we'd be visiting somewhere a little more exciting later on.

"Hope you don't mind that we came here. I know you wanted to go back to the city, but I just didn't want to drive all the way back," Ethan said, handing me a menu.

"Oh, no, this is fine." Had I known that going into San Fran was an option, I would've tried a bit harder to get us out there. "I guess we come here a lot?"

Ethan looked up from the menu, giving me a puzzled look. "The girls like to come here. Anthony spoils them."

"That's right." I closed my eyes and looked down at the menu.

"Harley," he started, placing our menus down, "are things…okay between us?"

"Um…" I honestly had no answer to this. I had no idea what was going on. "What do you mean?"

"Look, I know the fight we had last week was…well, it was bad. I didn't mean anything I said. I love you." Ethan grabbed my hand and circled the table to my side of the booth, sitting down next to me. Hearing him tell me he loved me was both awkward and sweet at the same time.

"I love you too. I'm sure I can put whatever it was in the past," I said. My new mission was to find out what was going on between him and me. He leaned in and kissed my lips softly before returning to his side of the booth. Ethan was a great kisser and my mind began to wander—if he was a great kisser, was sex going to be just as amazing? Quickly picking up the menu to hide the fact I was blushing, I skimmed over some of the items.

Anthony returned to the table and set down a bottle of red wine and two glasses. "What will it be tonight? The usual?" he asked.

"I think I'm going to have the chicken primavera," I requested. Both men looked at me, surprised. "That's my usual, huh?" I laughed.

"Harley, you went vegetarian four years ago," Ethan pointed out.

"Well, this is slightly embarrassing. Okay then, make mine the garden veggie primavera," I said, chuckling nervously.

"I'll have the usual, Anthony." Ethan handed the menus to Anthony before he walked away, still confused by my order. "Harley, what's going on? Have you been drinking?"

"I wish I had," I mumbled.

"What?"

"Nothing. I'm not drunk. I just…I guess I was in the mood for some chicken. I guess it was a weird craving," I lied. I couldn't believe I had changed into a vegetarian. I made a mental note to grab a cheeseburger tomorrow after dropping the kids off at school.

"Oh, okay. I'm glad that we have an evening alone. Talking about work and such is always hard when the girls are around."

I nodded, sipping my wine. This man was

absolutely gorgeous.

"Harley, in my meeting, we discussed the possibility of taking on one of the top clothing industries under our company name."

"Really? That's amazing!" I exclaimed.

"It really is. There's always a down side for this, though. The hours are going to be long and I'm going to be missing a lot more dinners and family time."

"Oh."

"I don't like that you'll be home with the girls all the time, but this will mean more money and more opportunities for the girls." He reached for my hand once again, but our dinner arrived before he could continue any further. Was this what Donna was talking about? I married a workaholic. Who was I kidding? I was once in his very position, and I'd chosen work over kids and family any day. But now, it felt different being told work was more important than me. I began to stuff food in my mouth to overcome the urge to cry.

We didn't speak for almost the entire meal. I not only had to suffer without meat, but I overcompensated on the extra bread and almost drank the entire bottle of wine. The wine definitely had me feeling a lot better.

"Ethan, you are so sexy," I slurred as he helped me out into the parking lot.

He chuckled, leaning down to help me sit in the passenger seat. I grabbed the back of his head and pulled him into me, kissing his lips, hard. His hands combed through my hair, gently pulling it. "Let's get home," he breathed, pulling away. I nodded, and quickly put on my seatbelt.

Tonight, I was going to enjoy the perks of being married to Ethan Prince.

As we pulled into the drive, we could barely keep our hands off each other as we walked into the house. His kisses were so passionate. We bumped into everything as we trailed through the kitchen toward the stairs.

"Here, let me," he insisted, picking me up and carrying me all the way to our bedroom. I was impressed with how strong he was. He laid me down on the bed and leaned over me, kissing me again. "Harley," he breathed. "Wow, you haven't been this turned on in a while."

I suddenly remembered the lingerie that I had purchased at the mall and really wanted to wear it for him. "Ethan, wait. Wait," I begged, trying to push him away. "I wanna freshen up, and I bought you something."

He smiled widely and rolled over onto his side of the bed. "Okay," he answered excitedly.

"I'll. Be. Right. Back." I sashayed to the bathroom, grabbing the bag from the floor on the way. I pulled the little nightgown out of the bag and removed the tags. Unzipping the dress, I tossed it across the bathroom and slipped the silk material over my head. "You can do this," I whispered to my reflection in the mirror. "You're married to the man. You have two beautiful girls, so sex has happened. He's probably a pro in bed." I took several deep breaths and opened the bathroom door.

Ethan was lying on his pillow, wearing nothing but his boxers. His chiseled abs and chest looked incredible. I tried my hardest to walk sexily to the bed, but I looked like a drunk monkey. "Ethan, what do you think?" I asked seductively, modeling the nightgown. I didn't get a response, so he must've not heard me. "Ethan?"

I climbed onto the bed to find Ethan asleep. I nudged him a couple of times, but all I got was a snore in response. I sat down on the bed, disappointed. So *this* was the perk of date night. Early bed time and no kids. I laid down on my pillow and tried to close my eyes.

***

The next morning, I woke to the smell of coffee brewing and no sound of kids. I quickly opened my eyes with hopes of my life being back to the way it was. But I was still in the house. I let out a heavy sigh as I pushed myself out of bed and reached for the robe hanging on the door. Ethan was in the kitchen flipping pancakes. Not only had I married one of the hottest men I had ever seen, but he cooked too? I was willing to forgive the little mishap last night for all of this.

"Morning," he greeted. I waved as I walked into the kitchen. "I'm sorry for falling asleep on you last night. Work has been killer, and I guess…"

I held up my hand, stopping him. "You don't need to explain, I understand."

He stopped flipping the pancakes and escorted me to the table. "I made breakfast. Coffee? Orange Juice?"

I smiled widely. "Umm, both."

"I thought so. Here ya go," he said, setting a mug of coffee and small glass of orange juice in front of me. He quickly returned to the pan and scooped out two pancakes and slid them onto a plate. "Here's the butter and syrup."

"Can I get the peanut butter too?" I asked, taking a sip of the orange juice.

"You eat peanut butter on your pancakes?" he asked, surprised. He grabbed the jar of peanut butter from the cupboard and returned to me.

"Sometimes." I nodded, taking the jar from him. He set his plate down and took a seat next to me.

"Huh, I guess I never realized that in the years we've been together. What time do we need to get the girls?"

"I'll get them once I'm done. I need to talk to Liv anyway. Also, tomorrow, I'm meeting the little one's..." I paused, trying to remember his damn name, "...Leila's teacher for coffee. He's trying to organize a school dance and needed some help. I offered."

"Sounds fun," Ethan said sarcastically. "I'm going to go grab a shower." He stood up and kissed my forehead, then walked toward the stairs. I scarfed more pancakes into my mouth and tightened my robe, running out the door. I was sure I felt the eyes of several neighbors watching me run across the lawn and knock frantically on Olivia's door.

She swung the door open, clenching her head with the other hand. "What are you doing over here so early? I figured you two would still be doing the nasty."

"Liv, I need to talk," I breathed heavily.

"Mommy!" Leila shrieked, running around the corner into my leg. She squeezed it tightly, wrapping her whole body around my leg as I walked in. "Auntie Liv let us watch Sons of Anarchy. Can I marry Juicy?"

"Uh, sure. As long as you keep your hands off my Jax," I said, prying her off of me. "Can you go play with your sister? I need to talk to Liv."

She nodded and ran into the living room, where it looked like a tornado ripped through. Liv was in the kitchen mixing two Bloody Mary's. She handed me a glass and sat down on the barstool. "I'm not allowed to drink alone ever again," she vowed. "So, what's got your panties in a twist?"

I took a large chug of the drink and coughed. "Did Ethan and I have a really bad fight recently?"

She looked at me confused as she pondered. "Honey, did you have a lot to drink last night?" I gave her a dirty look and she held up her hands. "Harley, he forgot your anniversary. Well, maybe not so much forgot it, but didn't show up to the party you had spent months planning. How are you not remembering this?"

"He forgot?" I gasped.

"Well, it seemed that way. You tried to call, like, a hundred times. You had a bunch of people over to celebrate with you guys. I'm surprised that he's not castrated, to be honest," she said wryly.

"Wow, I was really upset."

"Harley, you were devastated. You thought he was cheating on you. When he finally showed up, you asked me to take the girls and you had a horrible fight. He went off on you about not

65

understanding work, and you lost it."

I began to tear up. How could this great guy not remember a major anniversary? I sipped on my drink in complete shock.

"Mommy, can we go home?" Cassie asked, walking into the kitchen.

"Uh, sure. Head on over, I'll get your things," I offered.

"Girls, remember what Auntie Liv said? What happens here, stays here. So no telling your daddy about our little SOA marathon," Liv reminded the girls. I shook my head and watched the girls smile widely as they ran out the door. "They're going to tell him, aren't they?"

"Hope not." I laughed.

"Har, don't dwell on what happened. You've been trying to move past it. Besides, what brought it up?"

"He asked if we were okay last night." I sighed.

"Oh. Well, did you at least have some hot make-up sex?" She winked, nudging my arm.

I glared at her. "He fell asleep! I don't even want to go into it."

"Ouch, nothing like adding salt to the wound. Well, go get some! Just make sure you lock the door—kids can't unsee some things."

"Shit, I forgot about that. All right, duly noted. Thanks, Liv." I leaned in and gave her a hug. I was glad that one thing really hadn't changed—I still had my best friend.

Chapter Seven

As I walked back to the house, I tried to remember all the great things that could come from this whole mess. So one night of intimacy didn't happen. It had happened at least twice in this life, so I shouldn't worry. I walked in through the front door and the smell of pancakes and bacon filled the house. The girls were stuffing their faces with over-syruped pancakes and Ethan was sipping on his coffee.

"Hey," I whispered, motioning him with my finger to follow me.

He set his coffee down on the counter and quickly followed me up the stairs. I tried my hardest not to giggle as we ran toward our bedroom. I pushed him against the door as he closed it and pressed my lips onto his. Hard. His lips were so incredibly soft and I wanted to melt right then. He lifted me up and carried me to the bed, gently setting me down. My legs and arms wrapped around him, keeping him close against me. I couldn't risk him disappearing on me.

I could feel his erection pushing against his pants and it made me want him even more. He seemed very well-endowed and I couldn't help but pat myself on the back. I had picked a good one. He breathed hard as he pushed against me.

"Daddy? Is Mommy with you?" A giggle came from behind the closed door. Ethan slowly began to push himself off me.

"Shhh," I said, pulling him back toward me. "If we don't make any noise, maybe they'll go away," I whispered.

"Harley, you and I know that's not true at all. I owe you big time. We'll have some fun tonight, I promise."

I sighed and nodded, letting go of him. He adjusted himself before he opened the door. "Hi, girls," he greeted as they ran past him.

The girls jumped onto the bed. "Mommy, can we go to Pizza Palace? Please?" Cassie begged.

I gave her a strange look. I had no idea what Pizza Palace was, but I knew for sure there was going to be pizza there and I wasn't sure I was ready to deal with that mess again.

"Maybe you should ask your dad," I said, quickly taking the pressure off of me. They both turned to see him standing near the door with his arms crossed.

"Let's go get ready," he said. The girls excitedly jumped off the bed and began to dance around. I'd never seen kids this excited about a pizza place before. "I'm going to get the girls ready, why don't you take a nice, hot shower," Ethan suggested, winking as he followed the girls out of the room.

After that mini make-out session, I was going to need a cold shower. Why would anyone want to marry someone so hot, have kids, and then not be able to have a minute of peace alone? I pushed myself off the bed and padded to the bathroom, sulking the entire way. I started the shower and as I undressed, I realized there wasn't any soap left on the dish. As I looked for a bar of soap to put in the tub, I found a small box stuffed into the back of one of the cupboards. I pulled out the box and found a small, red vibrator.

I blushed and quickly put the lid back on the box. I don't know why I was so embarrassed, because in my apartment I had at least two. I just never imagined I'd find one now. I felt the steam from the shower pouring out and I tapped on the box. He was going to give the girls a shower and told me to enjoy mine. It wasn't going to kill me to have a moment alone.

I pulled the vibrator out of the box and stepped into the shower. I began to hope that the little toy wasn't loud as I turned it on. Thankfully, it was only a small buzz and could barely be heard over the shower. Before I could have any sort of moment, the door flung open and Leila came stomping in.

Panicking, I tossed the vibrator across the tub only for it to bounce off the curtain and land on the floor.

"Mommy, Cassie was..." Leila picked the vibrator up off of the floor. "What's this?"

"Oh shit!" I shrieked. Ethan came running in the door. He looked down at Leila's hand and snatched the toy out of her hands. "Thanks," I breathed.

"I wanna see that! It was making a noise!" Leila begged.

"Why don't you go play with your sister and we'll be down in a few." Ethan closed the door behind Leila, who left pouting, and locked it behind her. I continued to watch him as he held onto my vibrator that was still buzzing in his hands. He slid his pants down and, in a shock, I quickly averted my eyes. "I think this is yours," he chuckled.

"Thanks, I…I found it under the sink. Oh shit, I didn't even grab any soap." I smacked my forehead and turned the vibrator off, setting it on the bathtub ledge.

Ethan headed to the linen closet and grabbed a bar of soap, then stepped into the shower with me. His whole body looked so incredibly toned, his abs were well chiseled and as he moved into the water, the droplets seemed to glisten on his skin. He was a freaking god. "See something you like?" he said with a smirk, watching me as I stood there with a gaping mouth.

"Well, now that you mention it," I replied, trying my hardest to sound sexy. He stepped out of the water, brushing up against me as we traded spots under the stream. My whole body tensed up, hoping he'd just push me against the cold wall and get all of this built-up sexual tension out while we were in the shower.

"Your mom called a few minutes ago," Ethan mentioned, killing any sexual mood I had.

"My mom?"

"Yeah, she said her and your dad will be over

later tonight. Did I miss something?"

I really had no clue. My mom and I had never really had a typical mother-daughter relationship and for her to be calling me, it was out of the ordinary. Even if everything else was out of the ordinary. "I'll give her a call when I get out. Did she sound upset?"

Ethan shook his head as he lathered the bar of soap across his pecs. "Not really. She's obviously still mad at me, though. I wish you hadn't told her what had happened."

It was already shocking that my mother had called, but the idea that she was living in the same state as I was was unbelievable. When I had first moved to California, my mom and dad thought it was a crazy idea and felt California was too busy for them. My mom and I had a nice relationship, but not one where I'd tell her private things. My dad was a busy man, always working. I never imagined him being the vacation type. All of this was so weird.

As I finished washing up, Ethan stepped out before me. Jesus, even his ass was tight. I looked down at my stomach and while it was flat, it needed some serious work.

"I'm...I'm sorry that I said anything to her," I said quietly. Honestly, I had no idea why I was apologizing, but thought it would clear some air.

He leaned in and gave me a soft kiss. "It's okay. Let's go have some fun at Pizza Palace," he said sarcastically. I was beginning to feel frightened about this place.

***

Soon after everyone finished dressing and I had put a bit of makeup on, we piled into the minivan. One thing I never imagined seeing was Ethan Prince driving a minivan. I had to hold back the chuckles during the entire drive. We pulled into the parking lot and I began to inspect the massive building shaped into what should look like a castle. Neon pink lettering read 'Pizza Palace' with an animated king eating pizza.

We started walking toward the entrance and I began to smell the cheesy grease. My stomach was currently wishing I had brought antacids. I could already tell this was going to be no specialty pizza. The girls became more excited as we opened the doors. They both ran inside, and the smell of pizza from six days ago with a hint of old plastic toys and children's feet smacked me in the face.

I looked at Ethan, hoping he would smell the same thing I was inhaling and would tell me we could leave. He smiled as he watched the girls get excited about the massive ball pit. I grabbed us a booth near the play area, hoping they served some sort of alcoholic beverages.

"Welcome to Pizza Palace, my lady," a young teenage boy greeted as I sat down.

"Hi, do you have beer?" I quickly asked.

"The royal king doesn't allow any sort of alcoholic beverages. Can I get you a Coke?" The sound of his monotone voice made me want to strangle him even more than him telling me there was no sort of alcohol.

"Coke will be fine. Umm, make it four." I had no

idea what to get everyone else, so best to get the same drink to keep it simple. He nodded and moseyed to the back. As I sat and waited for my soda, I couldn't help but watch Ethan play happily with the kids. The way all of their smiles were beaming across their faces as they played in the small jungle gym.

"You know, this place would make loads of money if they served a martini."

I turned quickly in the booth to find Donna sitting behind me. "What are you doing here?" I snapped.

"I wanted to check in on you," she replied, holding her hands up. "Someone is a little tense."

"Tense? Yes, I am. I'm finding out that my *husband* forgot our anniversary. I apparently planned this big party and he just didn't show up. My mom now lives in the same state? She's also coming over later? I haven't had sex in a while and every chance I get to have a little fun, something happens to destroy that possibility." I took a deep breath, "Yeah, I'm a little tense."

"Well, on the bright side, you and your mom are speaking," Donna said. She pressed her fingers to the corners of her mouth as if she were trying to signal for me to smile.

I shook my head and crossed my arms. "If I'm not happy here and this wasn't supposed to be my future...why am I still here? Am I supposed to learn something from this? That's it! I'm being punished!"

Donna pulled a vodka shooter from her purse and quickly did a shot. "No," she said while coughing. "This isn't a punishment. It's just a mistake that I can't correct—yet. You still have some sort of feelings for Ethan and are obviously attached to the girls. *That's* what is keeping you here. Your *real* prince is out there, and you'll realize what needs to happen when you open your eyes."

"Do you have any more of those shooters?" I asked, changing the subject.

"No! You're in a children's play place," she scolded. I rolled my eyes at her and turned away. "Is it just me or does it smell in here?"

"Right?" I agreed, turning to see she was gone.

"Right." The teen had returned and was looking at me like I was a crazy person. "Uh, do you want to order some pizza?"

"Yeah, just a large pepperoni." I suddenly remembered the whole vegetarian incident and grabbed the waiter's arm before he could walk off. "Oh, uh, can you make that half pepperoni and the other half cheese? Thanks." I looked around for Donna, but there was no sign of her. If she could just disappear, why couldn't she take me with her?

"Mommy, I'm thirsty," Leila announced as she slid into the booth across from me. I handed her the small soda and she began to sip on it like she was severely dehydrated. "This is delicious!"

Ethan walked up to the booth with Cassie holding his hand and smiling. "This is so much fun," Cassie shrieked. She then gave Leila a strange look as she watched her guzzle her drink.

"Leila, don't drink all your juice," Ethan scolded.

"Daddy, it's not juice! It's pop! It's delicious. I want this all the time!" Leila rambled.

"Harley! You gave her soda?" Ethan quickly took the cup away from the Leila, who I was pretty sure she was going to bounce off the walls with the wide eyed expression on her face. "You know she gets hyper." Ethan gave both of the small kids cups back to the teen boy and asked for different drinks. I felt bad as I watched Leila begin to wiggle around in her seat. I prayed that she wasn't going to throw up with all that sugar and caffeine pumping through her system. I could only imagine what would happen if I gave the poor thing a Mountain Dew or a latte.

Ethan returned with two small cups of what appeared to be apple juice and sat across from Leila and me, next to Cassie. Besides the fact that he worked a lot, missed out on a party—well actually our *anniversary*—I wanted to know if there was a *true* flaw to this man, which Donna was so adamant about. We made beautiful kids, he had a killer body, and he obviously loved me. These were the thoughts that were keeping me here. I needed to find out more. More to this story, and why it wasn't meant to be my happily ever after.

"Did you call your mom?" Ethan asked, as the pizza arrived.

"Oh sh—. I mean, no. I'll call her after we eat." I noticed that before I even said 'shit' I got glares from all around me. I needed to learn to keep my swear words under control, at least around the kids.

"Harley!" I heard a shout come from the entrance of the restaurant. I set down my greasy slice of pizza and looked to see Gloria and Portia waving. I quickly waved back and slid out of the booth. "I see you brave this place too?" she asked sarcastically.

I nodded. "Yeah, I guess so. What brings you here?"

"This is where I meet up with Portia's dad. It's his weekend," she sighed. "Oh, I'm sorry I didn't realize you had the whole family with you."

"No, that's okay. C'mon over."

Gloria hesitated a few moments, and then followed me over. "Ethan, this is Gloria. She's Portia's mom."

Ethan choked on his soda, and stood up. "Gloria, nice to see you."

"You know each other?" I asked. Ethan looked up at me like he was a deer in headlights.

"No, uh, well, we met at the last school meeting," he stuttered.

"Well, I don't want to interrupt your family time. Besides, my ex should be here any minute. I'll see ya on Monday, Harley." Gloria hurried off with Portia and I sat down watching Ethan shove a bite of pizza into his mouth.

"Did I miss something?" I asked, trying to figure out why Gloria would leave so suddenly and Ethan act like that.

"Miss something? Like what?" His eyes widened and I began to realize he was hiding something, and I was bound on finding out what it was. I sat back and picked at my pizza, watching as the girls stuffed their faces. In the back of my mind, I hoped the girls would throw up the pizza; just to give him a dose of what I had to deal with the other night.

Then, I remembered my parents were making an appearance tonight. I wasn't exactly thrilled with the way this day was turning out. I definitely knew I was going to need a few glasses of wine later.

Chapter Eight

After a long day, the sound of screaming kids would be forever engraved into my head. I would never be able to get those shrills out of my mind. When we arrived home, I was the first out of the van and hurried into the house to wash my hands and anything else that was touched by the Pizza Palace. I ended up turning on the shower and stripping down. I figured my whole body was exposed to that germ cesspool.

"Harley?" Ethan asked, poking his head into the bathroom.

"Sorry, that place made me feel all sorts of itchy. I needed to rinse off."

"Well, your folks are here," he sighed.

I quickly poked my head out of the shower. "What do you mean they're here?" I panicked. "I thought you said later on tonight!"

Ethan shrugged his shoulders as he handed me my towel when I pulled back the curtain, then shut off the water. I could hear my mom's nasally laugh filling the house. I cringed at the thought of her judging me for every sort of décor in the house. My dorm room in college looked like I had one of the interior designers from a makeover show come and invade my space. I had to have everything a certain way or some Feng Shui shit.

"Oh, God," I whispered, wrapping the towel around me. "Please tell me that my dad isn't trying to tell jokes," I begged.

"He started as soon as he walked in the door." Ethan patted me on the shoulder and left the bathroom. I dried off and quickly dressed to save the rest of the family from any sort of further torture from my dad's humor.

The poor guy. My dad had been trying to be funny for as long as I could remember. The whole moving of the thumb trick…yeah, that was what he was famous for. The small town I was from enjoyed it and he always thought he would be a hit. However, he didn't realize the people he showed it to—old people at the retirement home—probably couldn't remember their own name half the time, so the trick never got old. Half his jokes were probably stolen from Johnny Carson and Jay Leno, but he didn't care. He would always claim he was just as good. I sighed as I heard the sound of my mom's laugh again. Tossing on one of my maxi skirts and a cami, I hurried downstairs.

Rounding the corner, I came down to see the girls snuggled up to my dad with him showing them what appeared to be polaroid pictures of some time in the past. My mom had a glass of wine in her hand and was watching some sort of program on the television. Well, at least my parents hadn't changed much in this life.

"Hey, guys!" I greeted, walking down the rest of the stairs.

"Oh, hi, sweetheart. I'm just showing the girls some pictures I found in the attic. I think this was your sixth or seventh birthday." My dad chuckled.

"Harley, have you seen this episode of this comedy show?" My mom pointed to the TV. It was some comedy battle to find the better comedian. I shook my head and walked toward the bottle of wine. "It's great, your dad and I have been watching it this season. Your dad thinks he can make it on the show." She snorted before taking a sip of her wine.

I sighed as I poured my glass of wine. Ethan was nowhere to be seen, so I took my glass over to the couch next to my mom and just stared at her. "Did you do something different?" my mom asked.

"Not that I'm aware of. Do I look different?"

"Hmm…maybe it's because the ass isn't in the room." She chuckled. I could feel my whole body stiffen up. My mom would never be one to call someone an ass out loud, and never in the presence of children. I glanced at the girls to see if they had heard my mother calling their dad an ass. Thankfully, they were too busy playing with their toys.

"Mom!" I shrieked. "Can you, just for tonight, I don't know…not be you?"

She took a long sip of her wine and then slowly put it on the end table. "Well, any man that forgets his own anniversary and doesn't have the balls to call…well, he deserves to have them chopped off."

"Mom," I sighed. "If he doesn't have balls, then

they can't be chopped off."

"Smartass," she chuckled. At that moment, Ethan returned to the living room. My mom rolled her eyes and went back to watching the TV, and I returned to the glass of wine. I could tell that one glass was not going to help the rest of the night. I quickly chugged the red wine and hurried to the counter to refill my glass.

"What's for dinner?" Ethan whispered.

"I can order us something. I'm not sure me cooking tonight will be a good idea."

Ethan rolled his eyes and reached into one of the drawers next to the fridge, pulling out a few to-go menus. "I guess one of these will do. Do you think your mom will need another glass of wine?" he huffed.

"At this point, I'm thinking we're going to need a couple of bottles." I sighed, then slurped the last little bit of wine that was in my cup. My mom let out a loud laugh and I could see Ethan cringe. I knew that men typically hated their mother-in-laws, but it was hard to witness it firsthand.

While Ethan went down to the basement, I called up one of the Chinese food places and ordered a ton of food.

***

Three bottles of wine. One container of Lo Mein. Three egg rolls. All of that was just me. And my parents still had yet to leave. Throughout dinner, my mom continued to make smartass comments toward Ethan, and to my dad about his jokes. I almost felt bad for the guys. During my high school prom, my mom seemed to grill my date, who was gay, about using protection. I was so embarrassed that I almost didn't go. However, tonight, I was a little drunk. I could only laugh after everything was said. The girls had already eaten their dinner and went upstairs to watch a movie.

"So, Ethan, how's work?" My mom sat back in her chair and crossed her arms.

"Well, Evelyn, things are great."

"Keeping really busy, then?" she pressed. Ethan nodded, and looked at her strangely as I continued to sip on wine. "I would hope so, since you ditched your own wife on her anniversary."

I choked on my wine. "Mom!"

She shrugged her shoulders. Ethan quickly stood up and began to put things in the fridge. My dad pushed his plate away from him and pulled at my mom's arm. "Evelyn, lets head home," my dad suggested.

"Bill, I'm just asking!" she whined.

"Mom, I'll call you later." I took her wine glass from her and set it on the table. "Thanks, Dad," I whispered as I hugged him. Ethan gave a brief wave as I followed them to the front door. "Have a safe trip home." I really wasn't sure where home for them was, but I hoped they made it there safely. I slammed the door shut and hurried back to the kitchen.

"I don't think I have to say it, but I will, anyway," Ethan seethed. "I'm not a fan of your mother."

I poured the last of the bottle of wine into my

glass and rolled my eyes, walking away. Truth was, I had never been a fan of my mother, either. However, the rule was that I was the only one allowed to talk shit about my mother.

"Ethan..." I began. I didn't feel like fighting with him. Trying my hardest not to stumble up the stairs, I walked slowly past the girls' room to find them passed out in their beds with the TV still on and the credits of *The Wizard of Oz* playing. I couldn't help but feel slightly sentimental, this was the movie I enjoyed most as a kid.

Sneaking into their room, I pressed the power button and then tried to sneak out. The Legos that were left on their floor had another idea. The stabbing pain shot up from the arch of my foot to the top of my head. I had never felt anything so excruciating in my entire life. I looked down to see a little pink square block sticking to the inside of the bottom of my foot. I would've thought I had stepped on hot coals, but this sensation was ten times worse.

"Mother fu—!" I huffed, trying my hardest not to spill red wine all over the carpet and wake the girls.

Hobbling out of their room, I limped all the way to my room. Ethan was lying in the bed, reading a section of the newspaper. "What happened?" he asked as he watched me limping.

"Legos," I breathed. I set down my glass and began to massage my foot. Ethan set down his newspaper and scooted closer to me. He spun me around in the bed and grabbed my foot from my hands.

"Let me," he insisted, rubbing my foot. His strong hands felt amazing as he massaged hard into my foot, moving slowly up my leg. Once he reached my knee, he grabbed my other foot. "I'm sorry," he whispered.

Even though it looked like it had pained him to apologize about being annoyed with my mother, it was rather nice. "Well, I'm sorry too. She's been that way my entire life."

Ethan's hands moved up both of my legs and grabbed my hips, pulling me down the mattress closer to him. "I love you, Harley," he breathed onto my neck as he leaned in and began to softly kiss my skin.

"Mmm…" I replied, feeling the goose bumps cover my body. Ethan slowly pulled my cami up over my head and tossed it onto the floor. His lips returned to my chest and moved along my navel.

He sat up, slowly pulled my skirt down my legs, and tossed it to the other side of the room. I giggled, letting out a single snort. He chuckled as I quickly covered my mouth, embarrassed. I had the habit of snorting when I became drunk. Ethan pulled my hands away from my mouth and began to kiss my lips. I may have been slightly drunk, but his kisses completely intoxicated me.

"Wrap your legs around me," he commanded, sliding his pants down. I was so excited this was actually going to happen. To finally feel him. He thrust into me, and I could honestly say that I was beyond impressed with his girth. I arched my back and moaned as I reached for him, pulling him closer. "Oh, Harley," he whispered. He moved slowly back and forth and I was becoming more anxious for the excitement to happen.

"Faster!" I begged. He began to speed up a bit as I dug my nails into his lower back. I wriggled underneath him, looking up at him. Ethan was biting his lip, trying to look away from me. I furrowed my brows as I began to lay still.

"Oh, shit," he groaned and thrust twice more into me. "Harley that was truly…wow…" Ethan rolled over to my side and looked rather impressed with himself. I laid there and grabbed the sheet to cover my body, trying to figure out if that moment was for real. Was sex with my prince always this…short? Did he actually think that was amazing? Dear God, please help me.

Chapter Nine

The next morning, I awoke to my alarm chirping, getting louder by the second. "It's Sunday," I whined, reaching for my phone. I looked at the screen to see it was a reminder for coffee with Matt this morning. I sat up, only to realize my head was still fuzzy from all the wine I drank the night before. Ethan was still sleeping when I stumbled to the bathroom.

Although a shower would have felt so much better than the splash of water I had just thrown on my face, I knew I wouldn't be able to make it to the coffee shop on time. I tossed my hair into a bun on top of my head, which looked like a blonde bird's nest, but who was I really trying to impress? Especially with the massive pounding that was going on in my head right now.

I slipped on some jeans and one of Ethan's black t-shirts, which was a little too big, but seemed appropriate for the homeless look I was going for.

"Where are you going?" Ethan yawned as I walked out of the bathroom.

"Coffee with Leila's teacher," I mumbled.

He nodded his head and turned over in bed. Had I not had to leave in the next couple of minutes, I would have tried to figure out if what had happened last night was the extent of our sex life. Granted, it only took that *one* time to get pregnant, but I wasn't sure the old me would have been able to call him back after a little stunt like that. What the hell was happening? I snapped out of my stare on his backside and grabbed my phone off the end table, hurrying out of my room. I crept by the girls' room, where they were still curled up in their blankets and seemed peacefully asleep.

As I hit the bottom of the stairs, I searched the living room for my purse. "Mommy?" a small voice asked from behind me. Screaming, I nearly jumped out of my skin as I turned around.

"Jesus Christ! Leila, you scared the piss out of me! I thought you were still asleep!" I panicked, grabbing my chest. I could feel my heartbeat racing away.

"I'm hungry," she replied.

"Well, uh, I need to go meet your teacher. How about you watch some TV and I'll bring home some donuts."

She nodded excitedly as I grabbed the keys off the table and watched her run to the couch, flipping on the TV. Now that I was pumping with adrenaline, I didn't think I was going to need that cup of coffee. That little girl had a great career as a ninja lined up.

As I started the van, I sat and looked at Ethan's car in the garage. Since we were married, he wasn't going to mind too much if I took it, right? I turned the van off, ran inside the house and grabbed his keys off the end table by the garage, then rushed into his car. The feeling of being in a sporty car again made me a little too happy.

I made sure not to speed, in fear of running into my repeat officer, but hurried to the coffee shop. Thankfully, it was only a few blocks away from the school, and I pulled into the parking lot to see Matt sitting next to the window, looking extremely good in his tight white shirt and glasses, which made me think I should have put a little more effort into how I looked.

I tied my t-shirt in a knot, to tighten it up a little bit, and quickly fixed my hair so it didn't look completely like a ball of knots. Sliding out of the car, I casually walked into the coffee shop. Matt looked up from the newspaper he was reading and gave me a smile and a wave. I pointed to the coffee bar and walked over to place my order.

"Can I just get a medium, black coffee and leave a little room for cream?" I ordered with the barista. She nodded and turned, filling up my coffee. I took the cup from her and gave my cash from my purse. I poured a small bit of cream in my coffee and wandered over to Matt. I was kicking myself for not giving a second thought on how I looked. Then I reminded myself, quietly, "You're married, Harley."

"Good morning," he greeted, slightly standing from his chair as I sat down.

"Ugh, not good yet," I chuckled.

"Rough night?"

"You have no idea. My parents came over, so that involved a lot of wine." I sipped on my coffee and savored the rich flavor. "You seem to be a morning person," I pointed out.

He chuckled and took a sip of his coffee. "You know, I'm not really. I just have lots of coffee."

I raised my cup to that response. "I'm really sorry about the other morning," I said. Matt raised one eyebrow. "For accusing you of...drugging my drink."

He nodded. "Ah, yes. Consider it forgotten. But can I ask a question?"

"Oh, of course!"

"What made you think that I drugged your drink?" He sat back in his chair as I searched my brain for some sort of answer.

"First of all, you probably wouldn't believe me..."

"Try me." He smiled and took a sip of his coffee.

"Well, I can honestly say there was this guy that looked like you at the bar that night," I lied. "I was still a little out of it and when I woke up the next morning it was just...it felt like I was drugged." I let out a sigh as he nodded his head.

"That's understandable. I do have to admit something," Matt said. "I felt a little weird the next morning. Like, the one beer that I had before bed— it seemed to make me a little fuzzy." I nearly choked on my coffee. "Are you okay, Harley?"

I nodded as I tried to clear my throat. "Sorry, went down the wrong pipe." I began to wonder if he was added to my mess by accident too.

"Let's talk about this dance," he said, changing

the subject. "I understand you have some marketing background."

I looked at him, surprised. I hadn't known much about him, but somehow he knew I had a marketing background. "Yeah! I do!" I exclaimed, blushing. I realized I had said that a little too excitedly.

Matt chuckled. "Any ideas, then?" He leaned toward me, and I got a whiff of his cologne and suddenly found that I couldn't think. The sparkle in his blue eyes began to entrance me and I couldn't talk anymore. "Harley?"

"Oh, I'm sorry. These kids are all about Disney characters, so how about something along the lines of a 'Happily Ever After' or 'Fairytale' dance. The girls can dress like princesses and the boys can go as knights or some of their favorite princes," I suggested.

"That's actually a really good idea! I do think, though, boys will tend to dress like superheroes," he laughed.

"Probably," I giggled. "Maybe, 'Fairytale-Superhero'?"

"That will be a lot of fun for the kids." He placed his hand on top of mine and I thought my chest was going to explode. His hands were so soft and mine were sweating underneath his.

"I...uh...yeah, it will be," I stuttered, pulling my hand away from his. After last night's big disappointment, I was sexually vulnerable. "I know a few places, if they're still around, that do some amazing decorations and signs." I pulled out a pen and started to jot down places on the back of a receipt.

"Awesome!" he said excitedly. "Let me know what this will cost. The school budget is limited, but I'm sick of them not doing anything fun for these kids. I'm paying for some of this out of my own pocket."

"Matt...that's really sweet of you," I swooned. Not many people would take money from their own bank accounts to pay for something like an elementary school dance. We continued to discuss the ideas of decorations and the possibility of holding a bake sale. I heard my phone ringing in my purse. "Sorry," I apologized, reaching for my bag. "Hello?" I answered.

"Hey, Leila said you were bringing donuts?" Ethan replied.

"Oh, shit, sorry. Yeah, I did. I'll head home now."

"Okay, see ya in a few." Ethan hung up, and I stood up as I began to gather my things. "Sorry, Matt. I guess I'm supposed to bring home breakfast."

"I understand. How are the girls?" he asked, handing me my coffee.

"They're good. I think Leila is going to have a wonderful career in the art of sneakery," I joked.

"Cassie is definitely going to be creative like her mom. After all these notes, she definitely gets her beauty and her brains from you," Matt replied, smiling.

If he continued with the sweet-talking, I was going to explode. "That's really sweet of you, thank you. I'll make a few phone calls in the morning and I'll have the prices for you after I pick up the girls."

"I appreciate it, Harley. Have a great rest of your weekend."

I waved goodbye and slid into my car. Matt stayed behind, then went back to reading the paper. He definitely was one of the sweetest men I had ever met. I backed out of the parking spot and began to drive down the road. I had no idea where a donut shop was, but I was bound to find one somewhere.

***

After driving around for nearly twenty minutes, trying to find any sort of place that had donuts, I found a little donut shop and ordered a dozen. I hurried home, pulled into the garage, and was greeted by Ethan looking less than thrilled that I was driving his car. The girls ran up behind him and began dancing around. They honestly looked like they didn't need any other sugar in their lives, but it was nice to see them excited to see me. Or the donuts.

"You drove my car?" he seethed.

"I'm sorry, but I thought it would be okay," I snapped as I walked past him into the kitchen.

"Mommy, you rule! Donuts are the bestest things ever!" Leila screamed.

"I want four!" Cassie announced excitedly.

"Four it is!" I agreed, pulling out plates from the cupboard.

"Cassie, you can have one," Ethan corrected. "Why did you drive my car?"

"Ethan, I didn't know you'd get so bent out of

shape! I'm sorry. I didn't want to drive that beast of a van. I miss having a car," I retorted. I wasn't sure why he was acting like this, but this was a side of Ethan I'd never seen before and I could honestly say I wasn't really liking it, at all.

"Well, you picked out the van. Stay out of my car."

"Geez, it was just down the damn road. Calm down." I grabbed the milk out of the fridge and slammed the door. I poured the girls a cup as Ethan stomped away, slamming the glasses on the table in front of girls.

"Mommy, don't fight. It's not nice," Leila demanded.

"When a guy is being a douche bag, don't let him get to you," I instructed. Both girls giggled. I walked out of the kitchen and down the hall when I heard Ethan talking on his phone in his office.

"I don't know. Look, things aren't as great as they seem. I'll see you in a bit." He quickly hung up his phone, and I backed away from the entryway and acted like I hadn't heard anything as I pretended to just walk down the hall.

He stormed out of his office, nearly knocking me down. "Oh, uh, are you going somewhere?" I asked, pointing to his tennis shoes that were now on and the gym bag on his shoulder.

"I'm going to the gym and I just got a call from work. I need to go in for a few hours."

"Ethan, it's a Sunday."

"Yeah, I know, Harley," he grumbled. "But if we want to keep this house, and they call me in—I have to go."

I crossed my arms and watched him walk past me. I could hear him say a quick goodbye to the girls as he hurried out the door. Padding back to the kitchen, I noticed their donut faces looking at me, confused. There was nothing to really say to them, I didn't even know what just happened.

Cassie looked as if she was going to start crying at any minute and I really didn't think I could take any of that right now. What do you tell a little girl? 'Sorry, your daddy is an asshole, possibly because of premature ejaculation.'

"Is Daddy mad?" Leila asked with a stuffed mouth.

"Probably. Hey, finish up. We're going to go hang out with Liv." Both of them looked at each other excitedly and shoveled more donut into their mouths. "Whoa, not that fast." I gagged at the sight of their mouths overflowing with donuts.

They each wiped their mouths and dusted off the massive amount of crumbs in their laps onto the floor. I was going to scold them, but right now, I didn't really care. I followed them to the front door, watching them slip on their princess slippers and smile up at me.

We walked across the lawn to Liv's house and all three of us began to knock on the door. She opened the door, covering her nightgown with her robe, her hair a wild mess. "Oh, shit, hey, Harley," she said, embarrassed.

"Wow, did we…interrupt something?" I asked, laughing.

"Uhh…well…not really," she started, leaning out the door. "Ken's here." Her face lit up and she was beaming.

"Hi, Harley," I heard a male voice call from behind the door. I was slightly excited to hear Ken's voice. He and Liv were really meant to be together.

"Hi, Ken!" I called back. "I don't want to interrupt, I just…I needed to talk."

"Oh, honey, come on in. We're done." She waved the three of us into the house. The girls ran up to Tabitha's room. I followed Liv into the kitchen where Ken was pouring a glass of orange juice. As Liv walked by, he spanked her playfully. She gave him a happy smile and sat down at the table. "What's going on?"

"Is Ethan cheating on me?" I asked bluntly.

"What?" she asked, surprised.

"You heard me. You are the nosiest person I know, Liv, and I mean that in the nicest way. Is he sleeping with someone else?"

"Thanks, bitch," she chuckled. I shrugged, because she wasn't going to argue it. "I personally think he is, but I don't know for sure. What brought this up?"

"I think that's my cue to leave," Ken chimed in. He walked over to Liv and gently kissed her lips, then smiled at me. "I'll call you later." Liv lit up like a Christmas tree and nodded quickly as Ken left the room, then hurried up the stairs.

"So, last night, we are finally having sex for the first time…"

"Honey, you have two kids. It's not the first time. Wait, you guys haven't been having sex?"

"No! We are finally getting it on and, Olivia, I shit you not when I tell you it lasted for only a moment."

"Please say it was actually more enjoyable than it sounds," she gasped.

"Nope. I was in shock!"

"So now you think he's cheating on you?" Olivia asked, sitting back in her seat.

I nodded and sighed. "Then this morning he got super mad at me for driving his car, got all huffy and said he got a call from work. Which, from the conversation, I'm not a hundred percent it was work," I sighed. "He told whoever was on the phone things aren't as great as they seem and he'd see this person later."

"Maybe something's going on at work." Liv paused, looking at me as I glared at her. "Hey, I guess I'm trying to play devil's advocate."

"Liv, you're supposed to tell me that he's a cheating asshole and I could do so much better," I whined.

"You're right. If you didn't have a marriage or children going on, I would. But it's slightly harder to just jump ship with all the Gucci baggage."

She was right. I wasn't even considering the girls or that I was a married woman. I couldn't just up and leave like I would when I had a horrible boyfriend. I had to either work things out or find out what was going on, despite whether this was supposed to be my life or not. "Yeah." I sighed. "I need your help then."

"Do I get to play spy?" she joked.

"Actually, you do! I want you to find out what's going on. I can't have him thinking I know, he might actually try to hide it more."

"You're funny, but I'll see what I can find out."

I was going to find out if Ethan Prince was really a prince or not.

Chapter Ten

Shortly after the girls and I left Olivia's house, I decided to actually try and get to know them a little more. Sure, they were my daughters, but I had no idea what they liked or what they even wanted to be when they grew up. I had no memory of them growing up, so I might as well get to know them a bit now. Olivia told me she had to run into the city, so she was going to try and follow Ethan. I started to feel bad about having Ethan followed, but I had to know.

"What do you girls want to do today?" I asked, drying their hair. I mentally noted that showers for two girls was messy—water was everywhere.

"Can we go back to Pizza Palace?" Leila turned to me and asked. I quickly shook my head, remembering the smell of feet.

"How about the park?" Cassie suggested.

"The park, I can do," I answered. We all left the bathroom and picked out clothes that were suitable for the park. Leila, as usual, fought me tooth and nail to wear a tiger costume, but today, I won. For some reason, this whole parenting thing was beginning to feel…natural. Actually, it was scary how everything seemed to flow today.

I decided the two of them had eaten out a lot the last few days, so, before we headed out, I made us a picnic. I could at least make peanut butter and jelly sandwiches, and the best part was—they didn't need to be cooked.

"So, where's the park?" I asked, opening the garage door.

"Mommy's gone crazy again," Leila said, twirling her finger next to her ear.

"Can we go to the one by the school?" Cassie asked excitedly.

I nodded and opened the van, placing the plastic bag of food in the front seat. I still had no idea how to work Leila's car seat, but I tried to help. After standing there, fighting it, Leila pushed my hands aside and clicked it into place. She gave me the biggest grin, with an 'I got it and you didn't' look. I couldn't argue.

We drove down the road and passed the school to find a massive park filled with screaming kids. The area had at least five slides, several swings, and many other random colored play-things. It was a kid's fantasy land, well, aside from Disneyland. There was even an area set up with a water play area with dancing fountains that reminded me of the Bellagio in Vegas.

"Yaay!" they both screamed in unison. My idea of a nice day at a park, with only a couple of kids and a nice picnic, turned into a nightmare. I was not ready to be around that many children. I took a couple of deep breaths and put the van in park.

"You guys, uh, be careful, okay?" I said, opening the van door. They both began kicking their feet in excitement as they unbuckled their seatbelts.

"We will!" Cassie shouted, pulling Leila behind her as they ran toward one of the playgrounds. I grabbed the food out of the car and wandered over to one of the tables that was closest to where they were playing. Had I known it was going to be this packed, I would have suggested something else. So much for getting to know what they were really like. I chuckled to myself, pulling out one of the sandwiches.

"Harley?"

I turned to see Gloria walking up to me, looking a little remorseful. "Hey! You got suckered into the park too?" I asked.

Gloria took a seat across from me, and nodded. "Beautiful day to be here too."

I looked around to see if her daughter was here. "Where's Portia?"

"With her dad. I was driving by and I saw you walking up here. I wanted to apologize," she sighed.

I set down my sandwich and quickly swallowed the tiny bite I had in my mouth. "For what?"

"I honestly didn't know that was your husband. And I promise that I would never…"

"Oh my God, you and…and Ethan?"

"No, no, it wasn't like that at all. I met him during a fundraiser at the school. I think you were either sick or with your parents, but he was trying to hit on me, and believe me—I'm not one of those moms."

"He was hitting on you? At the *school*?"

"Yeah, he said that he had seen me a few times and wanted to introduce himself. He thinks he's sly, but I told him that I was going through a divorce and I wasn't interested. He said he was going through one as well." Gloria reached over and placed her hand on my arm. "I had no idea that was your husband. If I had, I would have kicked him in the balls."

I couldn't believe that he was telling random people he was getting a *divorce*! The nerve of him! My mind was racing a mile a minute! I couldn't even wrap my head around it.

I chuckled. "Thanks. I appreciate you telling me."

"When I saw you guys at the pizza place, I was shocked. He had made it seem like he was heartbroken and really needing someone to talk to."

"He's going to have more than a broken heart," I whispered.

"I hope you and I can still be friends?"

"Oh, of course! I…" I was about to say more, but something over Gloria's shoulder caught my eye. "Gloria, do you know who those two women are?" I pointed to two women who looked like twins yelling at several children.

"Oh, the Knit-Whit Twins? That's Megan and Lana," Gloria snickered. "Rumor has it they had a bunch of money, but wasted it all. They got jobs, married the first guys they could get and popped out kids like crazy."

"I know them!" I gasped.

"You do? God, they don't even seem like people

you'd hang out with," Gloria said, surprised.

"I didn't like hanging out with them. They always made me feel…well, poor. It's kinda nice to see they put on some weight and have..." I paused, counting their kids. "Five each?"

"And Megan is pregnant again!" Gloria laughed. "Seriously, you are such a great person. I hope you nail Ethan's balls to the wall."

"Yeah, don't worry. I will."

"Well, I need to head out. I have some grocery shopping to do before Portia gets home. See you tomorrow?" Gloria began to walk toward her car.

"Yeah. Oh! Before I forget, do you know if any of these places are still around that create signs?" I asked, pulling out the list of places from my purse.

"Signs?" She looked over the paper and nodded.

"Yeah, for the school dance. I'm helping Matt with getting some estimates on signs and marketing stuff."

"Oh, I used to do marketing. I used this place down on Del Mar, they did amazing work."

"You used to do marketing?" I asked, pulling her down beside me.

"Yeah, a long time ago, though. Why?"

"I knew I liked you. I used to be in marketing too! Anyway, I may need your help with this dance. I don't know if a lot of my contacts are still around."

Gloria stood up and shrugged. "Sure! I always miss going back. But it's no place for a full-time mom. It got too hard juggling kids and work. You know, the hours."

I slowly nodded. I had heard about women

having to leave early to pick up their kids, and I would always seem to look down on them for doing so. Now I felt a little bad.

Shortly after Gloria left, the girls came running over to the table. "Can we have lunch?" Leila whined. "I'm starrrrrving!"

I smiled and nodded. "Of course. Here." I handed her the sandwich bag with a warm peanut butter and jelly sandwich. Both of them began to take bites and smear jelly all over their faces. "So, uh, Cassie," I said, getting her attention. She looked up with more sandwich on her face than in her mouth. "What do you want to be when you grow up?"

She shrugged and then it looked like she began to think about it. "I want to be a teacher."

"A teacher? How come?"

"They just seem so nice to kids and…Mr. Garner is a nice teacher and I want to be one."

"Fair enough," I chuckled. "Leila? What about you?"

"I want to be a market person," she replied with her mouth full.

"Like work in a store?" I asked, confused.

"No, I want to do what you did. You made pretty pictures and had fun!"

My heart melted. I never considered myself a role model to anyone under the age of twenty-one, so for a child—my child—to say they wanted to be like me when they grew up was truly heart melting. I teared up. "Thanks, Leila," I said quietly, holding back any sort of tears.

"And I wanna be SpongeBob too. He's funny!"

she added. I rolled my eyes, but couldn't help but chuckle.

I knew this wasn't the way my life was supposed to go, but the one thing I knew was that I was going to miss both of these little girls if I went back.

***

The girls and I spent the rest of the afternoon at the park. It was so much fun to see how big their smiles would get from just playing with them. I never knew I could love two kids so much, especially ones that I had just met. We came home, and I attempted to be motherly and cook spaghetti for dinner. It wasn't so bad, but I knew I had some work to do. I did miss my 'other' life, though. I missed my shoes, my purses, and the ability to leave whenever I wanted.

After dinner, the girls showered as I fixed their lunches for school the next day and made sure their backpacks were ready to go by the door. Ethan had yet to come home and I knew that the old me surely would have panicked. However, it didn't bother me, because I now knew, just from everything that had happened in the last few days, he and I weren't really meant to be. What did bother me was the fact that I wasn't going to be able to see the girls anymore. Without Ethan, they weren't going to exist.

As I tucked the girls into bed, I kissed them both softly on the head and watched them breathe quietly as they fell asleep. Leila was cuddled up to my old stuffed animal and Cassie was hanging her head off the bed. As I left their room, the doorbell rang through the house. I jogged down the stairs and found Donna standing on the stoop. "Hello, darling," she greeted, pulling me into a hug.

"I think I figured it out," I stated, leading her toward the living room couches.

"Oh?"

"Ethan and I really aren't supposed to be together. He's been a player his entire life and he still wants to be. He would rather have a wife that does everything for him, have a perfect family and wonderful in-laws, but I've provided none of that for him. And maybe that's why he tried to find someone new."

"Well, it does seem that way."

"On the outside I feel like I try to be happy, but on the inside…" I breathed heavily, "I can tell he's not happy here. Like, right now, he's somewhere in the city, either at work or with someone else. And I can tell you, I'm not at all sad."

"I'm proud of you, Harley," Donna replied, clapping her hands.

"Now that I have this all figured out, can I go home?" I whined. "I know I got close to the girls today, but I wanted to know what they were like," I quickly added.

"Harley, it was never about getting attached to someone, it was about finding out your true path."

"That's the thing! I figured it out! I'm *one hundred* percent sure I'm not *supposed* to be with Ethan Prince! So why isn't anything happening?"

Donna turned more toward me. "Don't worry, it's coming up. I want you to know who you're

105

truly meant to be with."

"I can't just go home and figure that out? I mean isn't that what dating is all about?"

Donna shook her head. "All right, darling, I just wanted to come by and say hi and see how things are going. What are your plans for this coming Wednesday?"

"What's on Wednesday?"

"Why, it's your birthday!"

With everything that had gone on the last week, I had completely forgotten all about my own birthday! "Oh my God! I forgot! Uhhh…no plans. Wait, if I don't have all this figured out by my birthday, am I stuck here?" I panicked.

Donna froze. "Honey, I honestly don't know." I began to take deep breaths in and out. "Harley, don't have a panic attack on me now! I'll figure it out," she said, rubbing on my back.

I glared up at her. "You are the worst fairy godmother, ever."

"So I've been told," she sighed. Donna helped me to my feet and I walked her to the front door. "Don't worry, I'm sure everything will get fixed," she reassured me as she left my house. As her car pulled away from our curb, Ethan pulled into the drive.

I crossed my arms and shut the door. Rather than having any sort of argument, I hurried upstairs to my bedroom. I tossed my clothes into the laundry basket, slipped on one of my nightgowns and crawled into bed. Not only was I exhausted from the day at the park, but trying to figure out what needed to happen to make my old life come back. Ethan peeked into the bedroom with a bouquet of flowers. "I know they're not white, but can this be my surrender flag?" he asked.

I smiled at the kind gesture. "Come on in," I sighed.

"I'm sorry about this morning. I got a call from Alana about the Tipsy's account and I guess things aren't going as great as we thought. They seemed to be pleased with us before, but now, I don't know what I'm going to do. I had to go in and try to come up with new ideas." Ethan fell onto the bed, exhausted.

Suddenly, I couldn't tell if the call earlier was truly about work or if he was lying. I thought the feeling of guilt would start to build up, but after the conversation with Gloria—I still had no remorse about wanting things between Ethan and me to be done.

"So, you feeling a little frisky?" he asked, snuggling up to me.

"No, not really." I yawned. "Long day with the girls and I need to get up early in the morning to take them to school." The fact that I was turning down Ethan Prince was just as shocking as me being a mom.

"Uh, okay," he responded, confused. I turned over onto my side and slowly fell asleep. Finding out that I might actually be stuck here was emotionally exhausting.

Chapter Eleven

I woke up ten minutes before my alarm, which rarely ever happened, even when I had to work. I think it was the excitement of planning an event, even if an elementary school dance was the reason for the early morning adrenaline. For once since I had been here, I was fully showered before the girls had even had a chance to get out of bed.

As I began to brew my coffee, Cassie came down the stairs. She was shocked to see me dressed and ready to go. "Morning," I greeted. "Hungry?"

"Umm…Did we miss school?" she asked, sitting down at the table.

"No," I laughed. "I need to meet with some people about your school dance. What can I get you? Something I don't have to cook. I don't want to get dirty."

"Cereal."

"One bowl, coming right up." As I poured a bowl, Ethan came down the stairs, adjusting his tie. "Hi, Daddy," Cassie yawned.

"Morning, Cassie. Harley, I have to work late

tonight, so go ahead and eat dinner without me. I gotta get this Tipsy's account fixed."

"Okay," I said, handing the bowl to Cassie. "I'm going to be working on the school dance, anyway. I get to put some of my marketing skills to work," I said happily.

"Well, don't have too much fun," he said wryly. "I'll see you later."

I nodded, and waved him off. Leila soon appeared in the kitchen. "Did we miss school?" she asked, looking me up and down.

"I actually showered. Yes, I know, it's a shock." I laughed. "Breakfast?"

She nodded her head and sleepily walked over to a chair next to her sister. I didn't bother asking, but poured her a bowl of cereal as well. I was ready to get on the road and start making calls. I couldn't believe I had given this up; I was looking forward to working again.

While the girls ate their cereal, I enjoyed my coffee and began to make mental notes of all the people that I had worked with on previous events—since things had changed, I hoped they were still around—and who I could call to help me get everything set up. I grabbed a piece of paper and made a list of all the ideas that Gloria could help me with. Sure, I was going overboard with the whole planning, but I finally felt like I was back to my old self.

"When you guys are done, go get ready. I need to get you to school on time, I have so much to do today," I instructed.

"Like what?" Cassie asked, handing me her

bowl.

"Your school is going to be having a dance on Wednesday. I'm helping Mr. Garner plan it today."

"What kind of dance?" Cassie's face began to light up. "Can I wear my ballet shoes?"

"This dance, you both get to dress like…princesses!"

Both girls squealed and Leila rushed over to my leg, squeezing it tightly. "This is the best ever!" she squealed.

"Leila, it's not until Wednesday," I said.

"Awww. I wanna dress like a princess today!" she whined.

"Maybe after school. Cassie, go help your sister find something that actually matches, please." Cassie nodded and led her sister up the stairs. I picked up the home phone and dialed Olivia's number.

"Woman, you know it's only seven, right?" she answered, yawning.

"Doesn't Tabitha have school?"

"She goes to school over by her dad's house. Anyway, what's up?"

"I thought about it last night, I want to cancel the mission. I really couldn't care less," I sighed.

"*What?*" she screeched. "He's your husband. If he's cheating, you deserve to know!"

"Liv, I have a plan and I don't want to know, okay? Please, just leave it. I love you."

I could hear her heavy sigh on the other line. "All right, if you know what you're doing…"

I smiled widely. "I do. I promise. Can you do me one more favor?"

"Sure!"

"Can you accept my apology for having anything to do with you and Ken falling apart?" She tried to interrupt, but I quickly spoke again. "I always thought you were the perfect couple and you guys deserve your happily ever after."

"Thanks, doll. I appreciate hearing that. But why...why the sudden change of heart?"

"Because I'm not the same person anymore. I've learned a lot over the last few days." I could hear her snickering, but for once, she didn't have anything smart to say after. "Good. Now, I need to make sure Leila isn't trying to wear a princess costume. I'll call you later."

"Harley?" she asked.

"Yeah?"

"You deserve a happy ending too. Don't let Ethan bring you down. He was once your Prince Charming."

"I know. However, I think this fairytale got all sorts of messed up," I chuckled. "I'll talk to you later." We hung up and the girls came down the stairs, thankfully with no costumes or mismatched outfits included. "Ready to go?" I asked, grabbing my keys.

They both nodded, and grabbed their backpacks. I was feeling rather on top of things this morning. I helped Leila into her seat, but still had no idea how to work those damn straps. She buckled herself in and I hurried into the driver's seat.

As I drove down the road, I noticed the same police officer off to the side of the road running the radar. I wasn't sure how fast I was going, but a huge sigh of relief passed my lips when I didn't see the familiar lights in my rearview mirror.

"All right, we made it to school without being pulled over or forgetting anything!" I cheered happily, pulling up to the drop-off area in the front of the school.

"What about our lunches?" Cassie asked, checking in her backpack.

"Shit!" I knew today was going *too* well. I had even made them the night before. Whatever thought I had in my head about getting this motherhood thing down slowly drifted away. I grabbed my purse off the seat and grabbed the last few bucks of cash I had in my wallet and handed them to the girls.

"Thanks, Mommy!" Leila sang as she hopped out of the car. I followed them up to the school gate and waved goodbye as the two of them dashed up the front stairs.

"Morning," Matt said quietly, startling me. "Oh sorry, I didn't mean to scare you."

"No! It's okay." I chuckled nervously. Man, he looked incredible and smelled just as good. "My mind is in twenty different places this morning. I am trying to plan my attack on the city."

He laughed, taking a sip from his coffee mug. "Well, I appreciate your help." I smiled as we both began to stare deep into each other's eyes. Suddenly, the sound of the school bell jolted us. "That's my cue to get in there."

"Yeah…have a nice day." I said, smiling as I waved goodbye. Watching him, I turned to get in my van.

"Hey, Harley," Matt hollered to me at the top of

the stairs. I turned to see him smiling. "You look really nice today."

Immediately blushing, I stumbled backward into someone behind me. The words couldn't escape my mouth to thank him before he went inside.

"You've got it bad," a woman said, helping me to my feet. Gloria was giggling as I spun around.

"I...What?"

"You've got it hot for teacher! But, hey, I'm not judging," she said, winking.

"Oh, hush. I do not. He's just..." I paused, sighing heavily. "Let's get to work!"

***

During the rest of the morning, Gloria and I spoke with nearly every business in the area about donating either food or money to sponsor the school. We went in thinking there was no way they were going to help out, but came out winners. Gloria and I raised over two thousand dollars for the school decorations and food, and Gloria pulled some strings with her sign designer office. They agreed to handle the entire signage for the dance. Overall, the martinis we decided to enjoy at lunch were well deserved.

"This was, by far, one of the best days I've had in a long time," Gloria said as we clinked our glasses together.

"I've missed work so much this past week. It felt good to get back out there."

Gloria gave me a puzzled look as she sipped her drink. "Week? I thought you'd been out since the girls were born?"

"Oh, yeah, I have. Did I really say week?" I stuttered. Gloria shrugged her shoulders and began to look over the rest of the checklist I had created for things we needed to get done. I was safe on having to explain anything and looking completely crazy.

"So, all we have to do is handle food and drinks?" Gloria asked, changing the subject.

"That's it! I was just going to suggest we get the whole bake sale thing to happen…"

"Harley?" A woman interrupted me as she walked by our table. I turned to see one of the women from my presentation for the Tipsy's account. "Alana," she reminded me.

"Oh! Hi!" Unfortunately, I really didn't remember her. I remembered seeing a woman sitting at the other end of the table, but I was so enthralled with Ethan that day—I barely remembered what I said. "I hear you are opening your third location!"

"We are. And I was really hoping you would have been there to help out. You really made everything so lively and organized. That bumbling moron that has taken over our account…" She began to blush. "I'm so sorry. I for—forgot."

I held up my hands, stopping her. "No, it's fine. I'm the one who should be sorry. I really wish I could have been the one to help."

"Well, I was hoping you'd say that. I've been talking with my business partners and we'd like to offer you a job. We heard you've been out of work for a bit, but hopefully we can talk you into coming back?"

My eyes widened and I swear my jaw dropped to the floor. Gloria kicked me under the table as I sat there in awe of the whole situation. "You…you what?"

"She wants to offer you a job." Gloria laughed.

"Alana, I'd love that. However, I don't know how long…" I stopped before I said something dumb. "May I think it over?"

"Of course!" Alana exclaimed.

"Actually, Alana, I'd wonder how much room you have on your team?" I asked, looking at Gloria.

"Help me out here—I'm slightly confused by the question."

"This is Gloria Vasquez. She's also in marketing and I think she'd be a great help to the team."

Gloria and Alana shook hands. "Is it a two-for-one kind of deal?" Alana asked. I nodded, and smiled at Gloria. "Well, I'll make sure I'm not going to be stepping on any toes, but…Gloria, send me your resume and I'll give you a call."

"Wow, thank you!" Gloria said excitedly.

"Let me know for sure, Harley," Alana said, handing over a business card before she started to walk away.

"That was so awesome of you," Gloria squealed.

"No problem," I replied, sipping on my martini. "Now, I have to come up with some way to tell Ethan he is getting fired from this account and I'm actually the one who is replacing him."

"Ouch. That's not going to be a pretty conversation."

I couldn't have agreed more. How do you tell the

guy that was once your boss that you are now taking one of his bigger clients because they think he's an idiot? I began to chug my beverage a bit more. More alcohol was going to be needed for this.

"Shit!" Gloria gasped, looking at her watch. "We gotta pick up the kids."

I whined, and set down my glass. I pulled out my card from my wallet, but Gloria snagged the bill from my fingers and paid with cash. We hurried back to my van. Today was, overall, a great day. I felt like my old self and my new self, rolled into one.

Just as we pulled up, the loud ringing of the school bell echoed across the street. "Thank you so much for your help today! I couldn't imagine doing that all by myself," I said to Gloria, giving her a quick hug.

"Harley, I had fun. I'm going to go email Alana my resume and portfolio now. I can't thank you enough. When is this dance, by the way?" she asked, chuckling.

"Wednesday!"

"Oh, shit! Yeah, there is no way this would have been all taken care of by then," she said, dusting her shoulder off. I laughed, and heard familiar squeals rushing toward us.

"Mommy! Can we dress like princesses yet?" Leila begged.

"Gloria, I'll call you later," I said as the girls quickly tried to pull me toward the car. Gloria nodded and waved as she greeted her daughter. I loaded the girls into the van and nonchalantly searched the schoolyard, not sure if I was truly looking for Matt, but it would have made a perfect end to the day to see his smile.

"Mommy!" Cassie called out excitedly.

"What's up?"

"I get to be the student of the day on Friday! Can you come to my class and hand out cookies?"

My heart suddenly dropped into my stomach. I had been constantly worrying about getting out of here, not once did I think about the things I would really miss out on. Or the fact that they really wouldn't exist. I slowly nodded, trying to hide the fact that my eyes began to water.

When we pulled into the driveway, Ethan's car was already parked in the garage. If my heart continued to sink, I didn't want to even think of where it could possibly end up. The day couldn't get any worse. Or could it? I slowly followed the girls into the house.

Chapter Twelve

While helping the girls get settled into the house, I realized that Ethan was nowhere to be seen. Granted, I hadn't really been looking, but he wasn't in plain sight. As the girls began their homework, I ran up the stairs to see him sitting on the bed with a bag packed. Just when I thought my heart couldn't go any further, it fell to the floor.

"Uh, hi?" I said, walking into the room.

"Hey. Harley, we need to…"

"Talk? Yeah! You have a bag packed!"

"Remember that clothing line the company signed?" He reached out and grabbed my hand, pulling me to sit next to him on the bed.

I slowly nodded, pulling my hand away from him.

"They want me to come to New York to take a look at some of their ideas," Ethan said excitedly.

"That's…great. But Ethan…"

"They want you to come too! It'll be a family vacation. We can stay a few extra days and do some sightseeing!"

118

I shook my head and crossed my arms. "Ethan, the girls have school. I just planned out a huge function for the school! Cassie is going to be student of the day on Friday. We can't just drop everything and leave the state."

"Harley, this is an amazing opportunity!" he argued.

"You're right. It is. For you." I was happy for him, but even in the short time I had been a mom, I realized everything was not *just* about me, anymore. I let out a heavy sigh. "Ethan, this is where *I* say we need to talk."

Ethan scooted away from me on the bed and looked at me strangely.

"Alana, from Tipsy's..." He nodded, crossing his arms. "She offered me a job this afternoon. She wants me to head up her marketing department. On site."

"What do you mean? She's using my company," he said, confused.

"Ethan, she's not happy. I don't know all the details, but I ran into her today and I can't pass up this amazing opportunity," I replied quietly.

"Harley, I want you to be home with our kids! You were just an assistant! She's crazy."

"For what? She was impressed with me when I pitched the first location, and if I remember correctly, they wanted me. Somehow, at some point, you took over. It's awesome that I got to be home with these wonderful little girls, but Ethan, you should've known how important my job was to me. I worked my *ass* off to get where I was!" I snapped.

119

"If *I* remember correctly, it was you always trying to get into *my* office and wanting to be with *me*!"

My stomach churned. "Ethan, before you and I say anything else we are going to regret..." I paused, holding back the tears, "...I think you should take the job. I think you should go out to New York. And most of all, I think you and I need to...I think we are done."

He let out a heavy sigh, and nodded.

"Ethan, I want to add that I really did like you. I would sit around the office and think what it be like to be with Ethan Prince." I paused for a moment, thinking about the day I met him and began to smile. "You were just so kind and always willing to help other people around the office. That's who I truly fell in love with." I sighed, and began to remember all the little things that had happened in the last week. "Then one day, I woke up and I realized I was actually married to you. Hell, I even had two beautiful daughters with you. You'd think that all my dreams had come true. Granted, it was weird, but it had come true. Then...then, I saw who maybe the real you was. You only care about *you.* I had really hoped this dream of you being this great guy wasn't just a dream."

We sat on the bed in silence for a moment. I hoped at that moment he would say something. Anything. However, he just sat there, silent. It was official—we were not meant to be.

"So when you say I wanted to be with you, I did. It was you that didn't want to work hard enough to be with me. And just for the record, not only did you forget our anniversary, you will be missing out on my *birthday*." I turned away from him, and then quickly turned back. "I do want to let you know, I did smell the perfume in your car *and* I know that you hit on my friend. Gloria? Yeah, she told me. You're a dog. If this was a fairytale, it's definitely not ending with a happily ever after." I stood from the bed, and handed him his suitcase.

Ethan slowly rose to his feet and walked past me without another word. The tears were there, but for some reason I didn't want to show him any sign of hurt. I could hear the girls crying for him not to go, but heard the garage door open a moment later. I rushed down to the girls as soon as I saw his car drive off from our window.

"Who wants ice cream for dinner?" I asked, scooping them both into my arms.

"Why'd Daddy have to go?" Cassie asked, wiping a tear from her cheek.

"Cassie, your daddy…he's got a job to do. He'll be back this weekend."

"Do you think he'll bring us a toy?" Leila asked.

I couldn't help but chuckle. "Probably."

"Can you make sure that you come to my class on Friday?" Cassie begged.

I squeezed her a little tighter. "Yes, Cassie, I'll be there." That was the moment the tears began to stream down my face. "Now, chocolate or vanilla ice cream?"

"Chocolate!" they said in unison. Chocolate it was. I was definitely in need of chocolate ice cream, wine, and my best friend. I pulled my phone from my purse on the counter and dialed up Olivia.

"Liv…" I sobbed.

"Oh, shit, what happened?"

"Can you come have ice cream and wine with us?" I begged.

"Harley, please say you're not giving the girls wine." She paused and could possibly sense the look I was giving the phone. "I'm kidding. Tabitha and I will be over in just a minute."

I nodded, knowing she couldn't see me, and hung up. A moment later, there was a knock at the door, and Olivia and Tabitha appeared on the front step.

It was so nice to be able to still have my best friend in this shit storm that had blown in. Olivia handed me a bottle of a Moscato and kissed my cheek. "It pairs well with ice cream," she joked.

I snickered as I followed her and the rest of the girls into the kitchen. As Liv scooped ice cream into bowls, I watched Cassie and Leila play with Tabitha in the middle of the living room. I couldn't imagine my life without kids now. The laughs, the whispers…It truly warmed my heart, and at this moment, I wanted this life, but the right way. Kids, but a husband that wanted to be more involved with us.

"What's on your mind?" Liv asked, pouring two glasses of wine.

"Do you believe in fairytales?"

"I do, but, honey, just 'cause this 'prince' was actually only a frog…"

"Oh, I'm not worried about that. I just…what if I told you that I was brought here by a fairy godmother that got it all wrong?" I couldn't believe

I was actually admitting to this, but I needed to get it out.

"I'd say, do I need to cut you off already?" She chuckled. I forced out a giggle and decided not to press it any further. I, instead, decided to enjoy a glass of wine and the double chocolate fudge ice cream.

***

Olivia and Tabitha left around eight o'clock, and by that time, I had already put the girls down for bed. The house, without Ethan, seemed so cold and big. I was suddenly more aware of all the lavish things that I was worried about, having all the brand names to keep up with my friends. Having the corner office and making money that would get me that apartment in the city. Now I was sitting on a king-size bed, surrounded by expensive linens, in an amazing home, but all I wanted was my small apartment with the few items that I skimped for.

One bottle of wine was obviously not enough to get me through the night alone, so as soon as the girls were in bed, I grabbed one more bottle for myself. I was slowly starting to feel like an alcoholic being here. I giggled to myself as I reached for the bottle on my nightstand, and accidentally knocked my phone to the ground. I picked it up, and pulled up my emails. For some strange reason, I had the urge to send Matt an email.

Dear Matt,
I didn't get to fill you in this

afternoon, but everything is taken care of for the dance! I'm so excited...It's going to rock.

Sorry for the late email. Me and Ethan just split and I'm drunk. Why am I even telling you this? I'll see you tomorrow. Man, how do I tell him I'd like to kiss those beautiful lips? That his eyes are so incredibly blue...Shit, what is this phone doing? I hope it doesn't...

Before I knew it my clumsy fingers hit 'send.' At some point, I had pushed 'dictate' and it picked up me talking to myself...out loud. I panicked, trying to figure out how to recall the email before he could see it. As I searched the settings, my phone beeped. An email.

"Oh, shit," I gasped. It was from Matt. I pressed the unread email and slowly began to read.

Hey Harley,

Sorry I missed you this afternoon. Kids and glue—they seem to think the stuff tastes good, but when their stomach hurts and they have to have help running to the nurse...Yeah, I won't go into details.

Thank you for all your help. I can't thank you enough. Gloria called the 'bake moms' and they called me. We will have a buffet

of snacks! You really are amazing.
I'll see you in the morning.
Matt

I breathed a sigh of relief when nothing of my epic fail was mentioned. I sighed too soon. Another email popped into my mailbox.

P.S. I'm truly sorry about you and Ethan. I know it may be a little soon, but I'd love it if you'd accompany me to the dance.

My heart stopped at that moment. One minute I was sad because I ended a marriage with my *husband*, and the next I'm finding myself flirting with the next guy. Then it dawned on me, was Matt my actual Prince Charming?

I wished I had a way to get ahold of Donna. If this was truly it, was this my way home? I laid in bed, trying to fall asleep, but everything was clouding my head. How would everything turn out if Matt was the one? But what if I was wrong, yet again? What if I was meant to be with the policeman that kindly let me off of tickets...*twice*?

Confused was never a word that described me, but in this last week, it was the *only* word that described me. What I needed was one more swig of this wine and to try to sleep all this off.

"Mommy," Leila whispered, walking into my room. I hadn't heard any sign of her walking down the hall or opening my bedroom door.

"Yeah!" I shrieked.

"I had a nightmare. Can I sleep with you?" she asked, climbing into my bed.

"Uh, sure." I really didn't have a chance to give her an answer—she had already cuddled into me and started to fall back asleep. I switched off the lamp on my nightstand and snuggled into my pillow. Leila's little ringlets tickled my nose, but her little sighs and small little fingers curling around mine made me realize that designer shoes or who the guy was didn't matter. I wanted to have a kid. And if this life really wasn't going to stick around, I knew what I truly wanted from my real life.

I slowly closed my eyes and began to finally fall asleep.

Chapter Thirteen

The sound of my alarm buzzing early in the morning scared the crap out of me. As I tried to reach for the annoying sound to silence it, Leila's tiny hand swung and landed across my face. "Jesus!" I groaned, holding my eye. How can one little hand inflict so much pain?

"Sorry, Mommy," she yawned, lying back on the pillow.

I padded my way to the bathroom to look at my eye and start getting ready. Today, I wasn't as ambitious to get all dolled up. The massive throbbing in my head, induced by sudden wine addiction, along with Leila's little fist of fury to my right eye began to all mesh together. "Oh, great," I sighed, looking in the mirror. My reflection startled me; I looked like I had a hard night, and the punch to the eye made it a little puffy. I hoped it wasn't going to turn into a black eye.

I splashed some water on my face and pulled my hair into a ponytail. As I walked out of the bathroom, I noticed Leila was no longer in my bed, which could only mean the girls were up and breakfast was to be made. I threw on some jeans and one of my t-shirts, and I could hear the girls giggling in their room. Walking by their room after I finished dressing, I saw both of them getting dressed and ready for school. Hearing their laughs was refreshing, especially after they just saw their dad leave last night. Thankfully, Leila was wearing something that didn't have to do with a princess dress. I hurried downstairs to start on some breakfast.

The thought of Ethan not even being here to help with the girls was disappointing. Seeing him leave last night really helped me realize he was not the nice guy he had pretended to be in the office. Always willing to help, wanting to help. He was not only a player in the dating field, but he also seemed to mislead everyone in that office. Thinking about it as I searched the pantry for something to eat just made me even madder.

"Why are you slamming the doors?" Cassie asked, sitting down at the table. I had no idea they were even watching.

"I'm going to start tying bells around your ankles so I know when you guys are coming closer," I joked. "I wasn't really slamming them, I was…never mind. Breakfast?"

"Can we have some eggs that aren't cooked really well? Just yellow?" Cassie asked.

Smartass. "Yeah, I can do that." I grabbed some eggs and a pan out of the cupboard, then concentrated really hard, at times a little too much, on making those damn eggs perfect. I couldn't leave here without making a nice breakfast.

I set the scrambled eggs in front of them and they looked surprised to see bright yellow, steaming eggs. "Thanks, Mommy," Leila said, smiling. I still wasn't used to the sound of being called 'Mommy.'

The girls finished up their breakfast, brushed their teeth, and we were out the door again. I felt like during my entire time here we were always on the go. The old me just worked and then went home. Sure, I went out a few times here and there with Liv and the twins, but I was now realizing that I didn't have much of a life. As I listened to the girls sing in the back to some song that was on the radio, I was impressed how much my life had changed having to care for these tiny people and keep them safe.

We pulled up to the school with a few minutes to spare, but I suddenly wished we were late. Matt was standing outside, greeting the kids as they entered the schoolyard. I thought I was going to puke in the passenger seat of the van. I had forgotten all about the email until I saw his bright smile.

"Okay, girls, I'm going to quickly drop you off. I want you to hurry out of the van. I can't stay," I instructed the girls as they looked at me like I had gone crazy, once again.

I pulled up to the school and reached back to quickly help Leila with her seatbelt. As Cassie jumped out of the van onto the sidewalk, she tripped on her own foot. She was definitely my daughter. I jumped out the driver's seat and hurried around the van to check on her.

"It hurts so bad!" she wailed. I helped her to her

feet and looked her over. There was a faint scratch on her knee, but other than that, I didn't see anything wrong. I saw Matt out of the corner of my eye, rushing over toward us.

"You okay, Cassie?" he asked, concerned.

She sniffled a few times before answering. "I think so, it just…I hurt my knee."

"You're not bleeding, I'm sure you're fine," I said. Matt gave me a slightly disappointed look. "But do you need anything?" I added.

She shook her head and grabbed her backpack off the ground. Leila stepped out of the van and hugged my leg. "I didn't fall," she pointed out. I chuckled at her as she ran off.

"That was an eventful start to the morning," Matt said, picking his cup of coffee off the ground.

"Yeah. Umm, Matt, about last night…"

"Oh, yeah, look you don't have to go with me to the dance, but I'd really like it if you could help me chaperone."

I think I was really falling for him, especially if he could avoid making me feel like a complete idiot and bringing up the things I had done. "No! I'd like to!" I blurted. "I just, well, I don't know what to wear." I smiled as his face lit up.

"Well, you can't go to the ball without a dress," he laughed. "Jonie's. The costume shop over on Third? They are helping some of the other parents get some costumes. Tell her I sent you over."

"Thanks, Matt, and for not…" I was interrupted by the sound of the bell.

"I've gotta go, but I'll talk to you later," he said, walking toward the stairs. It was official, he gave me butterflies.

Getting back into the van, I decided to head over to Jonie's to take a look at their selection. I drove in the general direction of Third and felt like a tourist as I drove slowly by each business. I finally reached the end of a strip mall where a small little sign read 'Jonie's Year Round Costume Shop.' I pulled into the parking lot and headed in.

As I walked into the small shop, I was surrounded by wall-to-wall costumes. Everything from Santa and Mrs. Claus to Freddy Krueger.

"Hello?" I called out.

"Be with you in just a second!" a voice from the back called out. There was hardly any room to move in the front of the store; I was surprised it wasn't a fire hazard. "Hi!" she said, peeking her head around a rack of costumes.

"Hi, uh, Matt Garner from the elementary school…"

"Oh, you must be Harley." She giggled.

"Yeah, how'd you know?" I asked curiously.

"He told me a few parents were helping and the rest of them had already been by. Come on back, I pulled all my princesses and prince costumes to the side. I'm Jonie, by the way."

"Nice to meet you."

Jonie guided me back to an open space with prince suits on one rack and large ball gowns on another. "There's a few that I have, but if you were thinking something else…" Jonie let her sentence trail off.

"No, I think I see the one I like." I walked up to a light blue dress that almost reminded me of

Cinderella. "Do you mind if I try this on?"

"No, of course, not!" She showed me to a fitting room and helped me take the dress out of the plastic garment bag.

I quickly undressed and slid the fluffy dress over my head. I began to think this was a little much for an elementary school dance, but hell, it was my birthday tomorrow and I was going to have fun. I zipped up the side and stepped out of the room. "Does it look okay?" I asked Jonie.

"Honey, you look amazing in that!"

"She's a modern day Cinderella."

I looked around to see who said that and could see Donna walking toward Jonie and me. "Donna?"

"You look beautiful," she said, getting teary eyed.

"Is this your mom?" Jonie asked.

"How old do you think I am?" Donna asked, crossing her arms.

Before Jonie could answer, I chimed in, "She's my aunt." Jonie nodded and walked away. I turned back to Donna. "What are you doing here?"

"Well, I heard through the grapevine—you and Ethan have split."

"How'd you hear that?"

"You do know I'm a fairy godmother, right?"

I nodded, rolling my eyes. "Yeah, he turned out to be kind of a jerk. Well, not kinda, he's a jerk." I looked at myself in the mirror and admired how well princess ballroom gowns looked on me.

"So you're going to the school dance?"

"No, I thought me and Liv would have a girl's night out and dress up in big dresses. She's going to wear her wedding gown. That dress has more taffeta and flowers than your worst bridesmaid dress, ever."

"Smartass."

I chuckled. "So, this looks okay?"

"Well, no dress would be complete without some glass slippers." She held up a pair of shoes from a table that were clear and resembled glass shoes.

"Thanks, Donna," I said, taking the shoes from her hand. For the first time since I had been here, I didn't really have the urge to ask Donna what was going to happen or when. I was happy just being here.

Donna helped me out of my dress, and then we said our goodbyes. I decided to run to a few different stores and find items for the girls to accessorize their princess dresses with. I was becoming a little excited for tomorrow night.

***

After spoiling the girls with tiaras, fake jewelry, and a lot of pink makeup, I hurried home to grab a quick shower before I had to pick them up again. There was not enough time in the day to do a lot of the things I wanted to do. However, I was able to enjoy a massive burger without being told I was a vegetarian. I savored every single bite of that juicy deliciousness.

When I arrived at the school, Gloria was standing outside. She was talking on her cell phone, looking extremely excited. As I walked toward her, she ended the call.

"Holy shit, Harley! I just got offered the job at Tipsy's and it's more than I have ever made in my entire life!" she squealed, pulling me into a hug. "I don't know how I'm ever going to thank you!"

A part of me felt horrible because I didn't know if she was really going to have this job when I made my wish for real this time. Making a wish to go back was becoming harder to think about. Things would definitely change, and now it wasn't just my life that was going to be affected. "Gloria, that's great," was all I could say. The ringing of that familiar school bell rang, and she pulled away from me.

"I can't wait to tell Portia. I've been working at the local supermarket, stocking canned goods. Her dad barely makes his child support payments and now, I couldn't care less! You have no idea how much this made our entire lives!"

"Hey, are you going to the dance?" I asked, changing the subject.

"Yeah, but you definitely won't catch me in a princess gown," she laughed.

"Well, I don't really brag about it, but it's my birthday and…well, I'd like you to come over and have a couple of drinks before the dance."

"Harley! I'll be there! In the last week, I really think you have become one of my best friends. Honestly, my only friend."

I loved Liv like a sister, but Gloria was definitely one of my new best friends. "Great! Dance starts at seven and I was thinking of having a couple of friends over for a drink around six."

"I'll be there, and I'll have food," she beamed

excitedly.

The girls ran out of the school and excitedly hugged me. "We can't wait until tomorrow!" Cassie screeched.

"Mama, can they come over to play?" Portia asked Gloria.

"Not tonight, but we have the dance tomorrow and we can go over after school." The girls whined a bit, but agreed. "Harley, thank you again. We'll see you tomorrow!"

I nodded and waved goodbye. "All right, girls. Let's go home. I have some pretty cool things for you."

"Presents?" Leila squealed.

"Yeah, they're for tomorrow. I thought you girls could use some fun stuff." Both of the girls began to dance and clap in their seats.

I had barely put the van into park, when the girls rushed out of the back and into the house. You would have thought I told them Christmas came early. As I stepped inside, I could see they had found the bag on the counter and they were overly excited about the jewelry and the tiaras. My phone began to vibrate in my pocket. It was an unknown number.

"Hello?" I answered hesitantly.

"Harley? It's Alana. I wanted to see if you had thought about the offer."

"Oh, hi! I did. I'd love to, but..." I paused, looking down at the girls. I knew I was about to make the biggest mistake of my life, but if I were to be stuck here, I don't think I could miss these laughs and smiles of these two little girls. "Alana,

Gloria is going to rock everything for you. I'm really honored that you picked me, but I have two little girls who are going to need me more than anything. I already missed a lot and I don't want to miss anymore."

"I understand," she replied solemnly. "Harley, we will always have a place for you here. If you decide to change your mind, give me a call."

"Thank you so much, Alana. I will."

I hung up, wandered over to the girls, and began to help them load on all the jewelry. Their laughter and hugs suddenly made me rethink everything that I had ever done in my life, especially saying I didn't want kids.

"Mommy…" Cassie started.

"Yes?" I asked, placing a second tiara on her head.

"I love you. You are the best mommy, ever."

"Me too," Leila chimed in.

My heart melted. I pulled them both into a hug and squeezed them tightly. I didn't want this to end. We spent the rest of the night dancing around and playing dress up. I made a rather tasty attempt at grilled cheese and paired it with some canned soup. Not bad for a pre-birthday dinner. Soon after dinner, the girls were so worn out they passed out on the couch. I carried them to their bed, dodging Legos like a pro, and then I headed to bed too.

Chapter Fourteen

"Happy birthday, Mommy!" Cassie and Leila screeched, jumping on my bed. It was only five thirty in the morning, but somehow the girls were already up. "We drawed you these," Cassie said, handing me a piece of paper. My eyes were barely cracked open as I took the piece of paper from their hands.

"Guys, it's only five thirty. Why are you up?" I whined.

"It's your birthday! We always get up early on birthdays!" Cassie said excitedly. Anyone else would have thought it was *her* birthday.

"Ugh, okay, I'm up." I yawned, sitting up in my bed. I rubbed the sleep from my eyes and tried to focus on the very colorful pictures the girls had drawn for me. "Wow, these are...what did you draw?"

"That's me and you. We are playing with balloons," Leila explained, describing the scribbles of colors.

"And this is me, you, and Leila. We are dancing

137

in the park," Cassie said, pointing to her stick figures with what appeared to be a park in the background.

"Wow, you did a good job, girls! Thank you very much."

"Can we dress like princesses today?" Leila quickly asked.

"Leila, the dance isn't until tonight…" I paused, watching the sad facial expression begin to form on her face. "You know what, what the hell. Go crazy."

Both girls jumped off the bed and ran for their bedroom. I laid back on my pillow. Another birthday, and again, I was single. I sighed, and contemplated if I was going to get out of bed or not. A ring at the doorbell jolted me. "Who the hell?"

Grabbing my robe off the back of my closet door, I hurried down the stairs. The sun was just beginning to rise, so I knew it couldn't seriously be a delivery person. I unlocked the door and was surprised to see Matt standing on my doorstep with a bouquet of flowers.

"Morning," he greeted.

"What are you doing here?" I gasped, taking the flowers from him. "I mean, thank you."

"Leila mentioned, well, several times, yesterday that it was going to be your birthday today. I wanted to be the first to wish it to you. But mostly, these are a thank you for all your help. The signs arrived last night for the dance and they're amazing. I don't think I could've done this alone. Thank you again."

"Matt…" I blushed. "Well, it was a lot of fun. As for being the first to wish me a happy birthday, you are two people behind." I laughed, smelling the flowers. It was a beautiful assortment of flowers: sunflowers, daisies, lilies, and one single rose in the middle.

"Darn it, I thought I'd beat them," he joked. "Anyway, I also brought you this." He reached to the side and pulled out a cup of coffee. "Thought you could use it."

"Aww, Matt, this is so kind of you. Thank you."

"Mommy, who's here?" Cassie called out from the top of the stairs.

"I'd better go," Matt whispered. "I'll see you later." He smiled, and jogged off to his car. Cassie reached the bottom of the stairs just as I closed the door.

"Those are pretty! Can I smell?" she asked, pulling my hand down to smell the flowers. She gave a big whiff and then ran off to the living room. She laid down on the couch and turned on the TV.

This was, by far, the best way to start the day. I shut the door and headed into the kitchen with my coffee, trying to find a vase to place the flowers in. As I started to search the kitchen cupboards, the house phone began to ring.

"Hello?" I answered.

"It's not even six a.m. and you had a gentleman leaving your place?" Liv gasped.

"You are the nosiest neighbor, ever! And you're right, it's not even six a.m., so why are you calling me?"

"I was calling to wish you a happy birthday, but I think you already had one." She chuckled.

"Liv...shut up," I laughed. "That was Leila's

139

teacher. I helped him with the dance that's happening tonight and he brought me flowers, that's it."

"Uh-huh, ask if I *really* believe that. Anyway, what are we doing for your birthday? I was thinking we should go into the city!"

"I…actually am going to the girls' dance. I—I told Matt I'd go and help him out."

"I knew it was more than birthday flowers!"

"Oh my God, I'm hanging up!"

"No, wait! Are we at least having a couple of drinks?" she asked, almost whining.

"Of course! Come over tonight around six. I'm having another mom, Gloria, come over and have a drink, too, before we go to the dance."

"Perfect! I'll see you later. Oh, Harley?"

"Yes, Liv?" I chuckled.

"Happy birthday!"

"Thanks. Talk to you later!" I hung up the phone and took a seat at the table. I had yet to find a vase, so I needed to be creative. I took a sip of coffee and looked around the living room. There was a porcelain book on the mantel over the fireplace and I wandered toward it. It was in fact a vase, but sat empty. Picking it up, I noticed the title of this little book was *Happily Ever After: A True Fairytale.* "How ironic," I said with a laugh as I carried it back to the kitchen to put the flowers inside it.

"How do we look?" Leila asked as she and Cassie began twirling around.

"Absolutely gorgeous!" I answered, loving how both of them were wearing princess dresses and tennis shoes. Cassie at least had matching socks, while Leila had one purple and one yellow sock.

I handed them each a Pop Tart, so they wouldn't make too much of a mess on their dresses, then sat back and enjoyed my coffee. I still had a little while to relax before I had to rush them off to school. Today, I was going to take it easy and go get my hair done. I wanted to feel like a princess if I was going to be dressing like one.

After enjoying my coffee for once, without having to run around, I took the girls to school. I hoped that I could thank Matt again, but didn't get a chance to see him. Once the girls were inside, I headed to the nearest hair salon. I was in luck when I found they did makeup and waxing too. I was in desperate need of a pampering day.

***

Even while relaxing, the day seemed to fly by. I was getting a little excited to put my dress on. Now I was aware where the girls got their overzealous behavior to dress like a princess from. My hair was in a tight, low bun and I couldn't have felt prettier.

I picked up the girls, and they couldn't stop staring at my hair and makeup. "You look pretty, Mommy."

"Thanks, Cassie," I beamed. "Wait 'til you see the dress."

We hurried home to get things ready for Gloria and Liv. Gloria had sent me a text message while I was getting my hair done, saying she was bringing a snack tray and a bottle of champagne. Liv had left me a message a few minutes later, telling me she didn't want me to put my dress on right away. Which, in Liv code, meant she was bringing over a cake and didn't want any to get on me.

The girls quickly finished up their homework, and at exactly six, Gloria rang the doorbell, Portia by her side, and Liv was right behind her.

"Happy birthday!" they both greeted in unison. Liv held up a cake box and tried to hide the top of it from me.

"No! You can see it in a minute. Do you have candles?"

"Uh, your guess is as good as mine. Maybe in one of the drawers."

Gloria set the platter of snacks on the table and hugged me before she handed me the bottle of champagne. "This is to celebrate our new jobs!"

"Gloria, I...I actually turned it down."

"What?" She gasped. "Why?"

"I think they will be satisfied with your work."

"But...they wanted *you*," she argued.

"They're happy with taking you on. Don't worry about me, okay!"

She nodded, walking to the kitchen in search of champagne glasses. Liv opened the box and, ironically, it was a cake with a princess and a frog on the top, reading, 'Happy Birthday, Harley, May All Your Wishes Come True.'

It then dawned on me, I had the choice of picking my wish today! As Liv lit the candles, everyone began to sing to me. I couldn't decide if I wanted to wish for my old life back or to continue living it this way. I was beginning to like my life the way it was going now. I took a deep breath, but before I could blow out Liv interrupted.

"Be careful what you wish for," she chuckled. "It might come true!"

I paused for another moment, and slowly blew out all the candles.

"What'd you wish for, Mommy?" Leila asked.

"She can't tell you, it won't come true," Cassie answered. I nodded in agreement.

While the girls enjoyed cake, I ran upstairs to quickly change. Carefully pulling the dress over my head, I zipped it up and slipped on my fake glass slippers. I tiptoed down the stairs, but once Liv gasped, everyone turned their head to me.

"Wow," everyone said in unison.

I blushed. "Thanks. So, who's ready to go to the ball?"

The little girls raised their hands and began to hurry toward the cars. Liv kissed my cheek and scooted me out the door. "I'll clean up. You girls have fun!"

"Thanks, Liv."

I followed Cassie and Leila into the van as Gloria and Portia climbed into her SUV. Stuffing a ball gown into a minivan was quite amusing. Thankfully, I didn't have to drive very far. We pulled into the parking lot of the school and I hurried to get out, so I could both breathe and make sure my dress wasn't completely wrinkled. Cassie and Leila hurried inside and I made sure not to be true to the shoes and lose one. It wasn't even near midnight and I felt like I was going to fall out of the damn things.

We walked down the long hallway of the school.

There were drawings of princesses and castles along with superheroes throughout the hall. It smelled like paint, glue, and something from the lunchroom was still lingering from lunchtime. I followed the girls into the gym. As we walked in, there were banners all around making the gym look like it had transformed into a castle. There were superhero cookies and pink cupcakes with little frogs on the top. I was truly impressed with the way everything had turned out.

A few parents were dressed up, talking to other parents as I looked around the room. Matt was in one corner talking to another adult. He was wearing black slacks with a cream jacket. Dear God, he was dressed up as Prince Charming. We made eye contact and I felt like my knees were going to buckle. He finished up his conversation and made his way toward me.

"Harley…you look beautiful!" he breathed.

"Thank you. You look very handsome," I whispered. A bunch of kids were running to where I was standing, and Matt quickly led me out of the way. I looked back and noticed I was standing near the dessert table.

"I didn't want you to get your dress dirty."

"I appreciate it. Jonie said this dress is a bitch to clean," I laughed.

The music was playing all sorts of Disney themes, which was wildly appropriate. I could see my daughters in the middle of the gym floor twirling their scepters and making their dresses flare up.

"Would you care to dance?" Matt asked, holding

his hand out for mine.

I placed my hand in his and nodded. He led me to the floor where the girls were dancing and wrapped his right hand around my waist, placing his hand on my lower back. My whole body flushed as he pulled me closer to him. "Beauty and the Beast" played loudly over the speakers and suddenly I felt like we were the center of attention.

"Harley?" I nodded into his shoulder. "I...The last week, I don't know what it is, but I feel so much closer to you. When you told me you and Ethan had split, I'm going to be honest and say I was kind of happy."

I pulled away and looked up at him. "Really?"

"Really."

We began to gaze into each other's eyes, still swaying to the music. He then lifted my chin and placed a sweet, soft kiss on my lips. We were interrupted by the 'ohhhh' of all the kids surrounding us.

I couldn't help but pull away and chuckle. "I think we have an audience," I whispered.

"I think so too. Would you like some punch?" he offered.

"That'd be nice. I need to run to the restroom. I'll be right back."

We parted ways and I left the gym, fanning myself. As I searched for the restrooms, I could see a woman sitting on the window sill, sipping on some punch. Walking closer, just as I suspected, I saw that it was Donna. She was adding vodka to her punch and I couldn't help but laugh.

"Do you carry shooters everywhere?" I asked.

"Only when I need them. Happy birthday, dear," she replied, holding up her little cup.

"Thanks. So, I made my wish. Is it coming up?" I asked hesitantly.

"I haven't received my notice. If anything, most wishes happen at midnight."

I sighed. "Oh. Well, what if I wanted things to stay this way?"

"What? I thought you wanted to go home?" Donna gasped.

"Yeah, but...Donna, I like everything that is going on. I never realized how much I wanted to have kids until those two little girls came into my life. Their laughs alone made me forget the fact that I could've been sad about Ethan walking out. Or how forgiving they were when I burned their damn eggs." I chuckled. "The guy in there, Matt, he's in there dancing with me to Disney songs and dressed up like Prince Charming. Everything about him is amazing. He makes me feel great about myself, and is even willing to laugh off my stupidity."

"Harley, you don't belong here. This is not for you. This wasn't supposed to be your life and you have the chance to go back."

"I know." I sighed. "I know."

"Well, I hope this time your wish works." Donna held up her cup again. "Have a wonderful rest of your birthday, Harley."

"Thanks, Donna." I leaned in and hugged her tightly. As I turned to leave, Donna disappeared, so I walked down the hall and headed into the bathroom. I could feel tears begin to slowly roll down my cheeks. Wiping them away, I fixed my makeup and took a deep breath. "Calm down, Har, it's only a wish."

Returning to the gym, Matt greeted me with a cup of punch and a cupcake. "Happy birthday."

"Thank you," I chuckled, taking a bite of the over-frosted dessert.

We spent the rest of the evening dancing with the girls and watching the rest of the kids have fun in their costumes. Overall, it really was a great birthday. At the end of the night, Matt helped me carry the girls to the van. They had found a quiet spot to laugh and play, but ended up falling asleep.

"This is going to sound really creepy," he said. I gave him a questioning look. "But I'm going to follow you home so I can help you put them in bed."

"Oh," I laughed. "You had me worried for a minute. That's really nice of you."

He got into his car and followed me back home. As we arrived at my place, he helped me by carrying Cassie as I carried Leila. We put them in their beds, then headed downstairs.

"Thanks for helping me," I said, opening the front door.

"No problem. You have some amazing little girls," he said, moving closer to me. "Good night, Harley. I'll see you tomorrow?"

I nodded, and then he leaned in and kissed me softly again on the lips.

As I started to close the door he put his hand in the crease. "Can I take you on a date?" he asked. "I know you just split from your husband, and I'm not meaning a date-date, but maybe another day of coffee? I've always enjoyed talking with you and…"

I held my hand up to stop him. My heart melted, because I was basically just asked out on a date by a guy dressed as Prince Charming. "Of course." He kissed me once more, and I closed the door. I slipped the dress off and tossed it onto a chair in the corner of the room. I sat down on the bed and took a deep breath. I was too anxious to fall asleep, knowing that tomorrow could bring a whole new me. Or old me.

I slipped my robe on and walked into the girls' room, kissing them each on the forehead and covering them up. I padded back to my bedroom and laid my head down, slowly closing my eyes.

Chapter Fifteen

Good morning, all you early risers! How about a little Taylor Swift's "Today Was a Fairytale" to kick off your Thursday.

The sound of my alarm began to play the notes of her song and I slowly opened my eyes. I was back in my old apartment, surrounded by all my old things. Everything in its place. I quickly got out of bed and began to search for the girls. "Cassie! Leila!" I called out, but my tiny one-bedroom apartment was empty.

I sat down on my couch and began to sob. This was not the wish I had asked for, but Donna was adamant in telling me that my other life wasn't the one I was meant to have. As I sat on the couch, crying, my cell phone began to ring loudly from my bedroom. I hurried to the room to answer.

"Hello?" I answered.

"Where are you? I thought you were coming in early today to help me with my project," Lucy whispered.

"Lucy?" I asked, confused.

149

"Who else would be calling you this early? Just hurry and get here, please. I have a presentation to give this afternoon."

"Uh, yeah, I'll be there in a little bit." I hung up the phone and hurried into the shower. All of my expensive makeup was laid out on the counter. I peeked into the closet and saw all of my clothing still hanging there.

Maybe what I went through was just a weird dream, maybe what I went through wasn't even real. I quickly showered and rushed around to get ready. As I dressed in my designer dress and shoes, I started to miss those yoga pants I had seemed to live in. I grabbed my house keys and hurried out the door. For some reason, I expected to walk out of my apartment and see my minivan, but I only found that I was about a block away from the train station. Everything I had, the minivan, the kids, the home— they were all gone.

Hurrying across the street, I was lucky enough to catch the next train. During the entire ride, I kept an eye out for any sign of Donna. I just wanted to talk to her and ask her why my wishes seemed to go wrong. As the train pulled up to my stop, I only had two blocks to walk until I reached my building. Heading toward the main entrance, I saw the figure of Ethan Prince. My heart began to race. How were things going to be between us? He had basically left me with two kids.

I followed him into the building and felt the butterflies swarm as we entered the bank of elevators. "Good morning, Harley. How are you?"

"You're seriously going to ask me that?" I

snapped, turning to him.

"Excuse me? I'm sorry, was I not supposed to?" he asked in shock.

I then realized what I had said and began to blush. "I'm so sorry, Ethan. It's been a really weird morning."

"Are you still planning on coming to the dinner this evening?"

I nodded with a smile, but in the back of my mind, I was unsure I should go. Then it dawned on me, I needed to find Matt. "Matt," I whispered.

"No, it's Ethan."

"Not you, sorry, I'm thinking out loud." The elevator hit my floor and I hurried out without saying anything else to Ethan.

"There you are!" Lucy shouted excitedly.

"Not now, Lucy. I need to find something." I sat down at my desk and dumped my purse, searching for the number Matt had given me. I was looking for anything from a piece of paper to a business card. There was nothing but my wallet, a stick of gum and a few tissues. "Damn it!"

"What's the matter?" she asked, peeking her head over the cubicle wall.

"I'm...This is just...I woke up thinking things were supposed to be a certain way and now... they're not."

"Don't we all?" She sat back down on her chair and then popped up again. "Hey, my presentation was postponed until Monday. So we can work on it tomorrow, when you are feeling a bit better."

I nodded and turned in my seat to face the black-screened monitor. I tried to get my head on straight to start work, but I couldn't seem to concentrate. The phone on my desk began to ring.

"Harley Prin—I mean Simpson," I answered. I could see Lucy's forehead begin to lift over the partition. I couldn't believe I answered the phone like that.

"How are you feeling?"

"Donna?"

"No, silly, it's Olivia! Who's Donna?" she asked, confused.

"Sorry, Liv. I'm fine, why?"

"You had a lot to drink last night! You told the twins they needed to grow the hell up!" she laughed.

"Are you serious?" I gasped.

"Yeah, but it was funny. You should've seen the look on their faces. You would've been able to, had you not fallen over one of the chairs as you walked to the bar. That bartender you liked, he called you a cab and helped you out."

"Matt! He was real!" I exclaimed.

"Uh, yeah, he's real. Still poor, but real."

"You and Ken are still happy, right?"

"Of course. Honey, are you still drunk?" she asked.

"Promise me you'll never leave him for Xavier!" I begged.

"Harley, I think you should take some time off of work or quit drinking. Are you running a fever?" Liv began to sound panicked.

"I'm sorry, Liv. I'm fine. It's been a shit storm morning. Hey, do you know what time the Olive Room opens?"

"All right, now I know you need to get some help," she chuckled.

"No, no, I…never mind. Liv, I want to thank you for always being a great friend to me."

"No problem, sweets. Go home and get some rest, okay?"

I nodded, knowing she couldn't see me, but hung up. This day needed to end, now.

***

Somehow, I managed to get my head a little focused on my work. I worked on the Tipsy's launch and tried to figure out what else needed to be done for their party. I spent my entire lunch searching for a Gloria Vasquez in the area, but nothing was coming up.

"I'm heading out. Are you really going to dinner with Ethan?" Lucy asked, bouncing up and down excitedly.

"How'd you know?"

"Some girls in the break room were talking about it. You've apparently made some other women around the office a bit jealous."

"I did?" I chuckled. "Well, it's just dinner, I promise."

Lucy winked at me. "Yep, sure it is."

I wanted to argue with her, but there was no way that she would believe me. I watched her walk down the hall as Ethan walked toward me.

"Are you ready? The car is waiting downstairs for us," he said, holding out his hand. The dimples that I once adored when he smiled suddenly made me want to hit him.

I stood up and walked past him, ignoring his hand. "Yep, I'm ready."

We rode the elevator down in silence. I could sense him looking over at me, but I couldn't bring myself to look back. He guided me to the Town Car that was parked outside our building and held the door open for me.

"We're going to Jackson's Steakhouse," he instructed the driver. "Would you like any champagne?" he offered.

"No, thanks," I replied, holding up my hand.

"Harley, I have to admit, I've really admired your hard work and dedication these last several months."

"I appreciate that."

"You are definitely headed in the right direction. Before you know it, I'm sure you'll be sitting next to me on the board."

My heart stopped. "You think I'm going to make it as a board member?" I asked, shocked.

"I think so. Look, this stays in this car. Harold Thompson is looking to retire. We've been asked to scope out someone new and fresh to take his spot. I'm putting your name into the running."

"Wow, Ethan, I don't know what to say!" I shrieked.

He leaned in and tried to kiss my lips. "You don't have to say anything."

I pushed him away before his lips touched mine. "Ethan! What are you doing?" I shouted.

"Harley, I see you getting all flustered around me. I know that you have a thing for me, I mean what woman in the office doesn't, but I could see this working out." He leaned in again and I quickly pushed him back.

"Ethan, as long as I live, I will never get with you again. Driver, can you stop here?" The car quickly pulled over and Ethan took a sip of his drink.

"Well, you can forget that board position. Wait…again?"

I briefly froze, not realizing I had said 'again.' "Oh, Ethan, shut up! You can take this job and shove it!" I snapped, taking his drink from his hands and tossing it in his face.

I got out of the car and quickly began to walk in the opposite direction. I had only heard of Jackson's, but didn't know where it was or where the hell *I* was. I just started walking. A crash of thunder startled me and it began to pour down with rain. I looked back to see the y had already sped away and I was beginning to get soaked.

I took off my heels and began to run for the nearest well-lit building. I didn't care that my feet were hurting as I stepped on tiny pebbles, I just needed to get this purse and dress out of the rain. And fast. As I sprinted down the sidewalk, I guess I hadn't been paying attention, and plowed into a man. I ended up getting knocked down to the ground.

"Oh my God, I'm so sorry," I said, pushing myself off the sidewalk. The gentleman held out his hand to help me up.

"No, I think that was my fault," he said.

I looked up to see the face of the man that I tried

to tackle and the sparkle of his blue eyes made me step back. "You," I whispered.

"Hey! You made it home last night!" Matt smiled. I was so lost in the moment of running into him again that I wrapped my hand around the back of his head and pressed my lips hard onto his. As I pulled away, he looked like a deer in headlights. I felt so embarrassed that I had just kissed the poor guy out of the blue.

"Matt?" a woman asked, walking up to us.

"Oh my God, you're seeing someone. I'm...I'm so sorry." I quickly ran off. First, I was kissing a guy that technically I had only just met the night before. And now, I was wrecking a relationship. I needed a drink.

"Hey, uh...Harley!" Matt called out to me. I slowed down as his strong hands lightly grabbed my arm. "Wait!"

"I am so sorry, I really don't know...Look, if your girlfriend or wife is mad, please..."

Matt interrupted by kissing me. Hard. His lips were the softest lips I had ever kissed. As he pulled away, I tried to regain my footing. My knees were shaking. My heart was beating incredibly fast. "First, that isn't my wife or my girlfriend. She's a fellow teacher. We met up to go over some ideas for a school dance. Second, I'm glad that you kissed me. Last night, I really wanted to kiss you before you got in the cab, and regretted it all day today. Seeing you tonight, I felt like it...It felt like things were supposed to happen."

My heart went from full on racing to melting in two seconds. "You feel like this was supposed to happen?" I whispered.

"Yeah, I do. So, how about that cup of coffee?" he laughed.

I stood up on my tiptoes and kissed him softly. "I'd love to."

Matt led me down the road, about a block away, to a coffee shop that was open all night. He led me to a corner booth and ordered coffee for the both of us. Surprisingly, we ordered the same kind of coffee—black with a little room for cream.

"So, do you work full time at the Olive Room?" I asked, blowing on my drink.

"No, I have a friend who is a manager. He gives me a call when they're short-handed, so I've just been picking up a couple shifts here and there. I need to pay the last of this student loan off."

"What do you do then?

"I work at the elementary school down the road. I'm a first grade teacher, well, an assistant to the teacher. Once I'm finished with the grad program, I'm hoping to be the head teacher." He beamed as he mentioned what he did.

"I take it that you enjoy your job," I said.

"I love kids. The way they learn and just take everything in. I honestly can't wait to have kids of my own," he said, slightly blushing. I knew the feeling. After being a mom for only a week, I was ready to give it a whirl. Again. "What do you do, Harley?"

"Well, I *did* have a job in marketing."

"Did?"

"Yeah, my boss turned out to be a real jerk. Right before I ran into you, I threw champagne in his face and quit. In a Town Car."

"Wow."

"Yeah. Don't really have a backup plan, so I'm a little disappointed in myself, but I'm sure I'll find something."

"Fate has a funny way of working out."

"You can say that again," I laughed.

Matt and I spent the rest of the evening laughing and talking about everything we could think of. From pets when we were younger to dislikes of food. We had so much in common and it felt so right being there with him. At four in the morning, we realized he had to work in a few hours. He didn't want to go, and I didn't want that either, so we decided to see each other later that evening.

I knew as soon as I got home, I had finally met my real prince.

Epilogue

One year later

"Harley, we're going to be late!" Matt called from the bottom of the stairs.

"Sorry, I had to change...again." I sighed, running down the stairs. My stomach was in a ball of knots.

"Honey, it's going to be okay. I think this will actually help us out."

"I know, but what if..."

"What if what? She doesn't like us? There are about a million of them in this city. I promised you the best and so far, Yelp made her sound like the best."

"All right. Wedding planner it is." I smiled and followed him out to the car.

Matt and I had been together ever since that night in the rain. We had been inseparable from day one, well, except when we had to work. Not even twenty-four hours had passed after quitting my job, when Alana from Tipsy's called me and offered me a job. They were so impressed with my presentation that they decided not to pay a big firm who didn't really care about their needs and to hire someone who was new and fresh. Like me.

A week into my new position, the business began to boom for them. So much so, they decided to bring on one other girl. Strangely enough, I began to work with Gloria. We became instant best friends.

Today, Matt and I were on our way to meet with a wedding planner. Matt had proposed to me just a couple of weeks ago. He had taken me to Disneyland for the weekend and had gotten down on one knee in front of the castle. It was absolutely amazing. The best part, well, besides the fact he had asked me to be his wife, was that he had flown in my parents to surprise me.

With work booming for me, and Matt being nominated for the principal position, we wanted to get married soon, but there wasn't enough time in the day to try and plan. Matt surprised me, again, with this meeting. I couldn't love this man more, even if I tried.

As we drove down the highway, Matt calmed my twitching leg by placing his hand on my knee. "All right, I think this is it," he said, pulling up to a small little building in the middle of the city. He ran over to the passenger side and opened my door for me. I took a deep breath in as we walked up to the door.

As we walked into the small office, the front desk seemed to be empty. I was nervous we ran too late and she ended up leaving.

"I'll be right with you," she called out from a

back room.

"That's fine," Matt and I answered in unison. We took a seat on the small sofa in the waiting area and looked around. It seemed more like a home than an office. "Oh great! I don't remember her name!" I whispered to Matt.

His eyes opened wide. "Shit, I forgot to look before we left."

"You must be Matt and Harley," she greeted, walking toward us.

My jaw dropped open. "Donna?" I gasped, pulling her into a hug.

"Uh, wow. I don't normally get greeted like this," she said, chuckling.

Matt pulled me away and whispered in my ear, "I thought you didn't remember her name."

"I'm sorry…I…" I didn't even have the words to clear myself of this embarrassing moment.

"Honey, don't worry about it," she laughed. "Well, let's have a seat and discuss details of the big day!"

We took a seat in a back office that looked like another living room. I felt like I had seen some of the items before as I looked around. It was when I saw on her desk a porcelain book vase with the title *Happily Ever After: A True Fairytale* that I couldn't help but laugh.

"She's been a little nervous about coming out here," Matt said.

"Everyone is nervous about the big day. What kind of wedding are we going for? Classic? Nouveau? I just have one request, nothing like a dead people wedding. I had one last week and, oh

God, it was…well, let's just say it was a little too weird for my taste."

"Oh, nothing like that," I agreed. "I was thinking something like…"

"Fairytale?" she interrupted.

My mouth hung open. "Exactly."

She smiled and nodded her head. "You two…you look like the happiest couple on Earth. I don't think anything less than a fairytale would be appropriate."

We sat in her office for another few hours, going over every single detail, down to the color of shoes. This woman really had a knack for planning weddings. I couldn't get over the fact that, at one point in time, she had been my fairy godmother. It was quite fitting that she was actually a wedding planner.

"So, we can have this wedding ready to go in three months if you'll let me be your planner," she said, smiling.

"We'd *love* for you to plan it!" I exclaimed. We stood up from the couch and Donna pulled me into a hug. "Thank you so much! You have no idea how much you are helping us," I gushed.

She hugged Matt, and then looked at me. "It's my pleasure! I live for this."

"Donna? Do you know where the Jefferson file is?" a male asked, walking into the room. "Oh, I'm sorry."

"No, honey, it's okay. Matt, Harley, this is my husband, Carter," Donna introduced us. I turned to see a tall, stocky man and realized he was the officer that had pulled me over. He smiled at me, and all I could do was give a slight wave. I didn't want to embarrass myself any further. "You both have a lovely evening and I will get to work."

We began to walk out of the office and I turned to Donna again. "I really do appreciate this. I know you get this a lot, but I don't think I could have planned this, and honestly…I can't wait to marry this man." I was beaming at this point.

"I can tell you two were meant for each other. So don't worry about a thing." She patted me on the back, walking me to the front of the building. "Just think of me as your fairy godmother." She gave me a smile and a wink as she closed the door.

I gasped. She *was* my fairy godmother!

THE END

Acknowledgements

My dear friend, Ying. I value our friendship so much and I appreciate you spending hours online with me, bouncing ideas back and forth. We have been through quite a bit together and it means the world that you have stuck by my side!

Ashleigh. I don't know how to even begin to thank you. You have listened to me rant, cry, whine, and throw fits. You helped me with bits and pieces of this story and made it seem more realistic, especially when I couldn't get out of my 'mom' mode. I love you to pieces.

Paula, thank you for reading this book almost chapter by chapter. Especially when I said, *check this out*! You have your hands full at home and yet you still took time to help me out. It's appreciated more than you know.

Laura and Angela. You both tell me you love doing it, just to do it. But helping me out every day—you both are amazingly great friends. I am honored to have met you both.

Anisa, I can't forget about you. Thank you for picking up your phone and talking with me about everything for an hour or more before I got to the actual point. I'm honored to call you a friend.

Tonya. You are an amazing person. You take time out of *your* busy schedule to talk to me, to help me and give your wonderful input. You are an angel. I am beyond thankful for all your help. You have no idea how much you mean to me.

I wanna also say a huge thank you to my girls— Layne, Holli, Heather, Nicole, Steph, Sara, and

Orry (yeah, I know you're not one of the girls, but you listen just as well, haha) I know I only talk about writing—so thank you for listening.

Bloggers—you guys are awesome! I message you almost daily, bother you, nag you and beg. You still are willing to help me out. You guys have a tough job handling divas, such as myself, constantly messaging you for help, but in the end I can't thank you guys enough.

And last, but definitely *not* least...my readers. You guys are what keep me writing. I wouldn't be here without you guys (obviously), but it's the little things—the messages saying you liked what you read, the reviews—and your constant support. Thank you, Thank you, *Thank You*!!

About the Author

Michelle Escamilla is a married mom of two. She began writing just to pass the time, waiting for one of her favorite authors to release her upcoming book, but soon found a new passion. When she is not writing, she is spending time with her kids, husband or family. She lives in Colorado, where she loves the mountains during the summer months for hiking and would love to be on a beach during the winter months.

Facebook:
https://www.facebook.com/authormichellee

Twitter:
https://twitter.com/msescamilla

31448468R00110

Made in the USA
Middletown, DE
30 April 2016